THE EDUCATION OF IVY LEAVOLD

SIERRA SIMONE

To Ivy and Julian's earliest fans—thank you so much for taking a chance on corsets and parlor games.

CHAPTER 1

"$\mathcal{I}$ want you to be my wife," Julian Markham pronounced. Julian Markham: owner of Markham Hall and owner of my heart. And possible murderer of my cousin two months since.

Panic—swift and sharp—seized me, squeezing my rib cage, making my heart pound. All I could feel was how small the library had become, how low the ceiling was, and how I needed to get outside, away from this—from this overwhelming thing and this overwhelming man who summoned such strong emotions within me. Love and desire twined together within my panic, grating against the doubts, the worries, the incredulity.

His mouth twisted at the corners, amusement lighting along his eyes. "You look so surprised."

A sharp retort came to mind, but it never made it to my lips. *Of course I am surprised.* Surprised and flattered and terrified. For one thing, someone like me couldn't marry someone like him; he needed to marry someone in his social station, someone wealthy and distinguished. Surely he knew this.

For another, there were the frightening things I had learned from the polite police officer in Scarborough—that my cousin Violet had been pregnant when she died, that the baby was almost certainly not Mr. Markham's, and that the entire narrative pointed to Mr. Markham's guilt.

Practicality and fear warred with emotion, and I looked away so that he wouldn't see the tears pricking at my eyes. I tried to speak, but the words wouldn't come. The vise around my chest continued to squeeze and press.

A beat passed, then another.

"Wildcat," he said. "Say something."

"We can't marry," I said, and I couldn't keep the pain from my voice.

"And why can't we?"

"Because—" I was dangerously close to sputtering. "Because! It's not right!"

This I meant in light of Violet's death, in light of his role in it, that it wouldn't be right for me to place myself at his mercy when I didn't know if he had any.

But he misunderstood me.

"You want to be my mistress, but you balk at becoming my wife? You are more feral than I thought. Are you so afraid of being trapped?" He took my wrist in his hand, his thumb pressing against my pulse, and I vividly remembered the first night we met. "Haven't I shown you that some restraints can be freeing?"

He had. Oh God, he had. And just like that, lust spiked through me, all the sweeter for the doubt surrounding it.

Julian Markham. My poison. My forbidden fruit.

"It's more than that," I continued, trying to summon logic in the midst of the hurricane inside me. "Violet died only two months ago. We haven't been in mourning long enough to honor her memory—"

"We can remember her just as well if we were married as if we were not. And as for honor, she has no family left that I know of and neither do I. This choice is ours and ours alone. Honor be damned."

"But—" I didn't finish my thought out loud. *But what if you killed her?*

Suddenly, he was in front of me, kneeling on the carpet, his hands on my knees. "Every moment away from you today was a torment. All I could think about was the way your eyes looked when I fucked you by the stream. The way you run through the woods at night. The way you are so unspoiled by worldly things, yet so eager for pleasure."

There were tears burning at my eyelids now. I did everything I could to will them away.

"We fit together, Ivy. All my life I have been looking for you, you who are so wild and willing and yet strong enough to withstand even my fiercest urges. You are what I thought I saw in women like Molly, what I thought I saw in Violet. I've known this for a while—since our night here in the library perhaps—but I truly realized it last night after I couldn't find you. I *need* you. I need you in my life, completely and totally. I want to be the husband I was pretending to protect you for." His eyes searched mine. "Hasn't it been obvious? I love you."

"You do?" It sounded so weak, so insecure, but in that moment, I needed to know if he was telling the truth. I needed to know that he was as absolutely consumed by me as I was by him.

"You are perfection. You are made for me, with your independence of spirit and your resilience. I never have to worry about frightening you or breaking you. How could I *not* love you?" He grabbed my hand and pressed it against his chest. I felt his heart beating, steady and sure. "You belong in here, my love. You belong in my bed, in my house, and you belong there with the right to own me. To own my time and my attention. Say yes." He pulled my fingers up to his lips and began kissing them, one by one.

"I want to," I whispered. It was the truth, pulled from me almost involuntarily. God, how stupid I was!

"So say it." His teeth were nipping at the pads of my fingers now, nips that turned into bites, bites that turned into sucking.

I want to. So much.

He drew my finger into his mouth, and my breasts strained against my corset, my legs parting unconsciously. My protests about station and honor and the nature of Violet's death grew fainter in my mind, dimming like lamps being turned down.

He moved forward and brushed his lips against mine, softer than the touch of a feather. This—this offer, this love—was unequivocally what I had hoped for in my most secret of hearts, the dream I only dared dream alone in the bitter hours of night. I would be cruel to myself—and to him—if I let these weak worries pollute a chance at happiness. Officer Mayhew himself had said that there wasn't enough evidence to charge Mr. Markham with Violet's murder. Wasn't I making something out of nothing? Hadn't we both suffered enough?

His kiss deepened and my eyes fluttered open to see his face as he kissed me. His eyes were closed, but there was no mistaking the vulnerability and the need, a need that superseded the sexual.

Love.

He'd admitted it: he loved me. And I loved him. Of course I would say yes.

As if he knew what I was thinking, Mr. Markham slid a hand behind my neck, tilting my face ever so slightly upwards and letting his fingers trail down my neck. They plucked at the modest neckline, which rested against my collarbone, and finding no purchase there, they moved down to my waist.

My mind began putting away my worries, one by one, shutting them into a chest and nailing it shut. Arabella went in one, Violet in another. Honor, decency, fear for my own safety, disparity of station and wealth . . . They all slowly packed themselves away, ordering themselves in rows in some distant corner of my mind. I could worry about them later. Right now, there was only Julian.

He pulled me to the edge of the couch and raised my skirts so that my legs were exposed. He pulled away, as if truly noticing my dress for the first time. "Why aren't you wearing one of your new ones?"

"I didn't think you'd be home tonight," I said.

"The dresses are to be worn all the time, not just when I'm around. I want to know that you're wearing only the best, even when I can't see you. After we marry, I'll buy you so many dresses that you'll never have to wear the same one twice."

I started to protest, but my words were cut off when his fingers started tracing circles on my thighs. "I haven't said yes yet," I managed as his fingers crept higher, finding the edge of my underthings.

"What can I do to make you say yes?" he asked, leaning in to press his lips against my neck. "Anything you want, I'll give it to you. Money, jewelry, travels abroad . . . just name it and it's yours."

"I only want you, Julian," I said. "That's all I've ever wanted."

He made a deep noise at the sound of his name, and his kisses on my neck turned into fierce bites and sucks. I could not hide my desire now, spreading my legs as far as I could, desperate for his fingers to reach the part that most needed him.

But he wouldn't satisfy me, not yet. His fingers danced just out of reach, refusing to go any further.

"Say that you'll marry me," he said again.

"I still don't—"

His fingers stopped, and his lips pulled away from my neck, leaving it cold and sensitive. He stared into my eyes, his own not giving any quarter. He wouldn't let me skirt by on this; he wanted a firm answer and he wanted it now. He stood.

"Don't leave," I cried.

"Quiet," he said. He was directly in front of me, his hips at the same level as my head, and even in the dim firelight, I could see the way his erection strained at his trousers. "Take it out," he said.

I looked up at him, expecting to see lust but seeing only hard determination instead.

"Take it out," he repeated. I shivered—not in fear but in excitement.

I unbuttoned his trousers, tugging them down to free his cock, which was magnificently stiff, taking my time so I could admire him. Every part of him was so virile, so *male*, and especially this part of him, which was stone hard and without regard for anything but its own fulfillment.

"Touch it," he commanded, his eyes blazing down at me, and I did, running my fingers from the base to the tip, feeling the veins ridge under my fingers, feeling it jump as I caressed the sensitive underside. I remembered our time in the temple folly, how I had gripped him then, and I did so now, circling my fingers around him and sliding them gently up and down. I was rewarded with a hiss.

"Open your mouth, Ivy," he said, trailing a finger from my lower lip to my chin.

I hesitated. This was something new to us. I had an idea of where this was going, but what if I did it wrong?

"*Open*," he ordered again, his tone stern, and I obeyed without thinking, parting my lips. The smooth crest of his cock brushed against them once, twice, and then slowly pushed inside. I opened my mouth even more, allowing him farther and farther in, until he hit the back of my throat. My throat closed against the invasion, and I made a choked noise, but Mr. Markham didn't stop. He slid out and in again, his hand on the back of my head, his eyes on mine the entire time.

"There," he said. "See? You are already mine. You opened your mouth for me, and you've opened your legs for me. I imagine in the eyes of the church, you'd be wrong not to accept my offer at this point. You already belong to me, so why fight it any longer?"

He was right, of course. Why was I resisting? I'd packed all my worries with their murmuring voices away; there was nothing in between me and what I most wanted . . .

I pressed my tongue against the underside of his cock,

6

enjoying his groan as I did, loving the way his breathing grew faster and his eyes grew darker as he held my head and fucked my mouth. I closed my lips around him, increasing the suction, and reached up a hand to stroke the parts of him that weren't inside.

"Your mouth feels so good. So warm and so soft. Look up at me, darling."

I lifted my eyes once more, not breaking my rhythm. I sucked as hard as I could and cupped and squeezed as much as I dared, loving how powerful he looked at this moment, both hands now on the back of my head as he used me to chase after his own orgasm.

I felt him thicken even more in my mouth. "I'm going to come," he growled. "And you're going to take it. Because you're mine."

My only response was to suck harder, to tongue him more, and after a few more thrusts, he grunted, shooting warmth down my throat in long pulses that took more than a minute to start fading in strength. Once he finished, I let him slip from my mouth, and he swiftly buttoned himself back up with steady hands, the slight flush in his cheeks the only betrayal of what he'd just experienced.

Perhaps there was a hint of a pout to my face, because he said, "I'm not touching you until you say yes."

"You can't seduce me into marrying you." I knew I would say yes, it was on the tip of my tongue, but there was something incredibly arousing about his frustration, about his need to hear me accept.

He lifted me from the couch and deposited me on the large reading table in the middle of the room. He disappeared for a minute, and I propped myself up on my elbows to watch as he went to the desk and retrieved a pair of metal shears, which glinted dully in the light.

He walked toward me, and for a moment, all I could feel was the distinct fear that I was trapped alone in a room with the man who had been accused of killing my cousin and what if I was next? I shut that thought in another box. Mr. Markham wouldn't hurt me. At least, not in a way that I didn't want.

If he saw my fear, he made no mention of it. Instead, he put the shears to the hem of my dress and began cutting. I made a noise of protest, but a swift, sharp look from him made me stop. So I did nothing but watch as he destroyed one of the few things I had brought to Markham Hall, one of the few things I truly owned in this world.

"If I had my way, I would destroy all of these rags," he said. "They hide you. They dull you. You are too beautiful to wear such hideous things." The shears went *snip snip* and my fear starting melting into something lower, something deeper. They *snipped* up to my waist, and then Mr. Markham laid the shears down, took hold of the two edges, and ripped the dress right to the top, giving an extra rip to tear cleanly through the tired lace neckline. I wore only my corsets and petticoats now, the latter of which he removed after tugging the shredded dress off me and discarding it in a heap on the floor. My other underthings were cut away as well, until my legs and hips and sex were completely exposed, though my corset still bound my breasts.

"Oh the things I want to do to you, wildcat. Sometimes I have to remind myself that we have all the time in the world . . . but I'll be damned if I still don't want to spend every minute making love to you." He went over to an end table. "I want to eat your pussy until you can't think coherent thoughts and you forget how to speak. I want to play with you in public; I want to make you come at the dinner table or in the middle of a crowded ballroom. I want everyone in society to see how gorgeous you are when you're being pleased. I want everyone to see that pretty little mouth wrapped around my cock." He took a lily from a vase on the table. "But mostly I want to fuck you. I've fucked many women, Ivy, and I've never fucked one like you. Your cunt is perfect—did you know that? Hot and wet and so goddamned tight. And the way you beg for it, the way you snap between fierceness and frenzy—well, it's almost more than I can bear."

He walked back to me, holding the white lily. Its stem arced gently, weighed down by the large petals.

"I'm still waiting for that yes," he said.

"I know," I whispered, desperate from his words, and then froze as I felt the cool, silken skin of the petals brushing against my bare folds. After being so aroused with no stimulation, the sensation was almost overwhelming. My head fell to the side. "*Oh.*"

The flower swept up to tickle my clitoris. My toes curled.

"You're wet, wildcat," Mr. Markham observed. The flower left and then there was a sharp *flick* as it struck my clitoris. I moaned.

"Now," he said. "Will you say yes?"

I nodded.

"I need to hear you say it."

But I couldn't at that moment, because he bent down, his head between my legs, and I could feel his warm breath everywhere—on my thighs, on my sex, on my sensitive bud. My mind seemed to leak out information, leaking out everything I knew and everything I was, filled with only one thought: *I need him to touch me.*

He blew on me, and goose bumps raced up my arms. "Please," I said. "I need you."

"Not good enough," he declared, straightening. He undid his pants and pulled out his cock, which was hard again, hard and glorious, and I moaned once more.

"Please."

He stroked himself a couple of times, watching me as I watched his hand moving over that wonderful thing that I now needed with such desperation it left me breathless. Then he grabbed my hips and jerked me roughly to the edge of the table so that my legs hung off the edge and so that the tip of his cock was less than an inch away from my opening. I squirmed, trying to get closer to him, but he planted a wide hand on my stomach and pushed down hard enough that I couldn't move.

Then he did something unexpected and ran the head of his cock up my folds, from my wet entrance to my swollen clit.

"Oh Julian," I whispered. "Please."

"Say it," he said, with another rub against my clit. My body shuddered with need. "Say it or I swear to God, I'll make you watch me stroke myself. I'll make you watch as I come on that snowy white corset of yours, and then I'll leave you here to suffer alone."

One more rub, this time with his cock spending extra time pressing against my bud, and I finally caved. "Yes," I cried. "Yes, I'll marry—"

I hadn't even finished my sentence before he thrust into me. My back arched off the table, pleasure and pain lancing through my core and out to my limbs, out to my toes and fingertips. I felt every curve and crest of him and whimpered as he slowly withdrew to the tip, his hand still flat on my stomach. He bore into me again, slowly but not softly, his other hand coming around to grip my thigh. After he sank all the way in, he ground himself against me, rubbing against my clit, and my back arched again.

"That's it," he said. "Isn't it so much better this way? You'll be mine and I'll be yours. This cunt will be mine to fuck whenever I want." He continued slowly for a few more strokes, holding me still while he drove me wild with his restrained but inexorable pace. "So tight," he murmured, watching himself as he slid in and out. "So perfect."

There was something rawly erotic about surrendering my life to him, almost more erotic than surrendering my body. Would he really do those things he said? Make me come in public? Make me suck him in front of other people? The thought wound my body tighter than a drum.

"Julian," I said. Green eyes met mine. "Use me. Do those things you can't show anybody else. Please."

A flush crept up his neck. Without a word, he roughly flipped me over, so that my feet touched the carpet and I was bent over the table. He didn't miss a beat, just buried his dick in me again, a hand wrapped around my neck for leverage. This angle was so much deeper and his thrusts so much stronger that I realized I was making noises—mews, cries, moans—that were entirely out of my control. And then he used his free hand to caress all around where we were joined, his fingers getting as slippery and wet as everything else.

He slid a slick finger into a place I'd never imagined, and that deep place within me—the place Julian was now pounding repeatedly—surged at this new development. His finger moved, and I realized he was stroking himself from inside of me, using the pressure to make me tighter than ever.

His hand moved from my neck to my front, where he quickly found my swollen clitoris and began working it hard and fast. "I want to feel you come around me," he told me, his voice near my ear. "I want you to squeeze my dick with everything you have."

Between his driving cock, his fingers on my clit, and the one working in my tight hole, I could feel it building, like a storm, heavy and unstoppable. In fact, it almost frightened me. Everything in me felt too tight, too taut, and I felt brittle, like I would shatter if I stood before the oncoming waves.

"I'm scared," I whispered, and as the words came out, I realized they were about more than the pleasure threatening to break me.

"I know," came the deep voice of my lover. "But I'm not. I'll be right here with you."

And then another finger pushed into my hole. I made another noise, impossibly close now.

"That's it," Mr. Markham encouraged, the circles on my clit growing relentlessly rough. "Show me how you can come."

It started deep within me, near the head of Julian's cock, the muscles spasming outward so hard that tears pricked at my eyelids. It ripped through my folds, through my clitoris, through my backside; it tore up through my chest and down to my legs, seizure after seizure, clench after clench, and my mind abruptly switched to blackness, my only focus on the soaring surf that took my body. I was bucking my hips, trying to grind myself back into Julian and I was only distantly aware of the wild noises I was making.

Bit by bit, the waves subsided, leaving me breathless and quivering and acutely sensitive to the fingers and cock that still worked me. A second orgasm gathered itself within, whirling and swirling.

"I'm going to come inside you," Mr. Markham said, his words breaking into a groan. "I'm going to fill you with my seed. And when you're full of me, you'll remember that it's *me* you're marrying, *me* you belong to, and *me* that you love."

And then he gave a soft moan. "Yes, here it comes. Oh God, Ivy. I love you so fucking much."

A groan sawed out of his mouth and I felt him pulse hard inside of me, a never-ending heat and throb, and my body responded in kind. My second climax came at that moment, softer and milder than the first, but strong enough to milk him, strong enough to make me cry out again.

He was still coming, thrusting, and panting, and then with a shudder, everything about him stilled. We stayed like that for a moment, his fingers and cock still buried inside of me, our limbs limp and sated, my mind slowly flickering back into conscious thought.

He abruptly pulled out and flipped me over onto my back. He spread my legs with his hands, stepping back like an artist examining his work. I once again propped myself on my elbows, and I could see his cock, still glistening and erect, the occasional aftershock still making it jerk.

He used a finger to probe my entrance. "I wish you could see this, Ivy," he said. "It's beautiful. My cum spilling out of you. I want you to walk around every day like this, with my seed in your cunt, so that you will belong to me even if I'm not with you. Every day."

"Every day," I repeated, my voice hoarse.

He buttoned himself up, gathered a blanket from beside the sofa, and gently wrapped me in it. Once I was safely in his arms, he grabbed the shredded remains of my dress and carried me up to his bed, where he unlaced my corset and put me between the sheets.

"Can you promise me something, wildcat?" he asked, laying down next to me. "As my future wife?"

"Mmm?" The sheets were so soft.

His fingers touched my hair. "Promise me that you'll never ask me about Violet's death. About the night before it happened. Please."

"Why?" I managed to say. It was such a strange request, maybe even a disturbing one, but my mind was so heavy, so tired, and my soul was still singing.

His arms tightened around me. "Just promise."

If I had been fully awake and not fresh from being fucked senseless, then I would have been alarmed at this. Alarmed at the deliberateness with which he had waited until I was at my most vulnerable, my drowsiest. I would have wondered what he wanted to keep secret and why.

But I wasn't fully awake or fully aware—and maybe even if I had been, I would have promised anyway. Because I loved him. Because I wanted him to keep loving me. Because I didn't want anything to keep us from each other.

And I didn't want to believe that he could have killed Violet. His secret was something else, surely. He was ashamed that they had fought that night. He had said things he now regretted. It couldn't be anything graver than that. I refused to let it be.

"I promise," I murmured sleepily. I meant to say something else, about how I trusted him no matter what, but my mind seemed unable to compute even basic thoughts. Instead, I kissed his fingers as he brushed the hair away from my face, and I fell into a deep slumber as the worries rattled in their small boxes deep into my dreams.

CHAPTER 2

I woke from sleeping like a tree wakes from winter, unfurling my limbs and stretching, feeling promise and contentment in the future, though I did not know exactly why.

I rolled my face into the pillow, unbelievably soft, unfamiliar, and then my other senses came to life. I smelled the grass and sunshine smell of Mr. Markham, I saw the richly embroidered hangings above the bed, I felt the delicious twinges from bruises both inside and out—bruises I had begged for the night previous.

And then it came to me, all of the memories, all of the decisions, everything from last night: I had agreed to marry Mr. Markham. I had said yes.

I became aware of another presence in the room, and I looked over to see Mr. Markham sitting in a chair across the room from the bed, his long legs stretched out before him, his green eyes watching me like a predator watches prey. Intently. With ownership. But this observation didn't frighten me. At least, it didn't frighten me in the sort of way that would persuade me to avoid him. Rather, it electrified me.

He was wild and feral, like myself. We were the same—solitary animals forced into human skin.

I sat up and stretched some more, feeling muscles pull and complain in new, delicious ways. Ways that reminded me of how it felt to be draped across a table and used for pleasure.

Mr. Markham's mouth twitched, as if he knew what I was thinking. "Come here, Ivy," he commanded.

I slid off the bed and walked toward him. I'd been put to bed completely naked, and I remained that way, but I felt no shame. Indeed, I felt nothing but satisfaction when his eyes blazed at the sight of my bare breasts and hips. When I reached him, he issued another order. "Kneel."

I obeyed without thinking. Whatever he wanted, I wanted. *One flesh.* Wasn't that the wedding vow? We would be one flesh. And flesh cannot doubt itself. Flesh cannot deny itself.

"Good girl." He stroked my tousled hair. "You know, I half expected you to vanish in the night. To evanesce away like a phantom. Or a dream. I couldn't fall asleep for fear that you wouldn't be there when I woke."

I turned my face into his hand. "I'm here. I'll always be here."

His eyes burned once more. "Yes. Yes, I'll make quite sure of that."

The boxes rattled in the back of my mind, the deep fears and the knowledge that I had buried, but I ignored them and instead pressed my lips to the inside of his palm.

He made a noise of approval. "You are still willing then, to marry me?"

"Yes."

"And to have me teach you how to please me? And how to let me please you?"

"Yes."

He unbuttoned his breeches, keeping his eyes pinned to mine, revealing his stiffening cock. Without warning, his hand was on the back of my head and he was feeding it into my mouth, forcing me to open, to take him as deeply as I could.

He groaned. "Fuck, Ivy. That mouth. It's almost criminally good."

I loved it. All of it. The salty taste of him as he slid against my tongue, the way I could smell soap lingering on the skin of his stomach, the groans issuing from his mouth. His hand on the back of my head as he drove the pace. The way he didn't stop me when I used my fingers to caress him, to cup him, to dig into his thighs and hips and pull him closer to me.

"You are so eager to please. Look up at me—no, keep me inside your mouth as you do. Yes, that's it."

I kept my eyes up as I pleasured him, experimenting with flicks of the tongue and variations in suction, more aroused by his steady gaze and heavy, determined hand than I would have been by the enthusiasm and encouragement of any other man.

"You are so inexperienced, wildcat. I almost don't want to teach you. There is something—*ah yes*—you are able to stoke me to impossible fire with your fresh eagerness. Yes, just like that."

I brought my hand to his shaft and began pumping him in time to my bobbing mouth.

"Yes," he hissed, his eyes fluttering closed and his self-control finally ebbing away. "Suck it, pet. Suck hard."

His cock swelled in my mouth, no longer flesh but stone, every vein and ridge as hard as marble. I expected him to ejaculate right then, wanted it even, but my head was tugged roughly back.

"Get your dress," he growled. "Crawl to it."

It took me a moment to remember the garb of green lawn that he had cut away last night, to remember that he had brought it upstairs with us. He released my hair and I crawled over to the bed, where I saw the ruined dress crumpled on the floor. My sex felt exposed as I crawled, exposed and wet and hungry, and when I cast a look over my shoulder, I saw Mr. Markham staring at me with a look so predatory it bordered on ferocious. I grabbed the dress, eager to get back to him, but stopped when I saw something under the bed. It was a small chest of rosy wood, bound with bright golden hardware. Inlaid into the side was more gold—swooping letters spelling out AW.

Arabella Whitefield.

It must have been her chest, and Mr. Markham must have saved it. Not only saved it, but stored it under his bed, as if he didn't want anyone to find it. And the box gleamed and shone; it wasn't dusty. It was dragged out frequently then, dragged out and its contents lovingly viewed and cataloged. My heart squeezed at this unexpected devotion he showed his first wife.

"I'm growing impatient," he said darkly.

I turned away from the bed—and its tragic box—and brought the dress over to him, painfully aware of how tight my nipples were, how heavy my breasts felt as I crawled.

He sat still, as still and as composed as if he were at a formal dinner, his elbow braced on the arm of the chair and his head braced against his fingers as he watched me. But at formal dinners, men didn't sit with their trousers open, their rigid dicks standing at attention, pre-cum glistening at the top. But even as it throbbed, even as I saw Mr. Markham's pulse thrumming in his neck, he made no move to touch himself. He only watched, with hunger, as I presented my old dress to him.

"Spread your legs, Ivy," he said.

I did, feeling the thick hand-knotted rug slide against my knees, feeling the cool air kissing the wetness along my center. The ache inside of me tripled, and then tripled again as Mr. Markham impatiently kicked my knees farther apart. His cock pulsed, but still he refrained from touching it. I watched as a small droplet of pre-cum oozed down the silky underside of his dick, wanting nothing more than to lick it off, to lick him until he finally, finally, finally lost control.

"Not yet, wildcat," he said, guessing at the look on my face. But I couldn't look away from that part of him. It was so magnificent, so beautiful, and all I could feel was the emptiness in my cunt where it should be, stroking and rubbing me from the inside out. I wetted my lips and leaned forward and then my jaw was caught in his fingers, not bruisingly hard, but hard enough that a shiver of possession shuddered through me.

"I said, *not yet.*"

I tore my gaze away from his cock and met his eyes. They were as they always were—coolness warring with passion, pain warring with pleasure. Torture and guilt and shame, underscored by desires that he would never be able to deny himself.

Those eyes searched mine, asking questions and demanding answers.

Can I take from you?

Yes. Please, God, yes.

Satisfied, he let go of my jaw. "Are you wet?" he asked.

I nodded.

"Show me. Touch yourself."

Without hesitation, I ran my fingers over my clit, sucking in my breath as I did. I was already so aroused, so swollen, that I knew it would only take a moment's work to bring myself to climax. I pressed my fingers against it once more, circling and circling as hard and as fast as I could, my core already beginning to clench.

Mr. Markham caught my wrist in his hand. "No," he said sternly. "This is not for you."

My lips parted in surprise. He had, of course, denied me pleasure often in the past, but now that we were to be married, surely those obstacles that had held him back before were removed?

I should be upset, I realized. *I should be furious.* But God, that stern voice, that command. That implication that I was only here to be used, to be an instrument to bring him satisfaction.

It made me more aroused than ever. I trembled with the need for release, my nipples painfully peaked, my breath now shallow and panting.

"Put your fingers inside," Mr. Markham said slowly, deliberately, as if talking to a servant. "Put them all the way in."

I complied, unable to stop the small whimper that escaped me.

"Now pull them out."

I moaned now, missing even the paltry stimulation of those two fingers.

"Hold them up so I can see." He examined my fingers in the muted light, turning them this way and that, acting oblivious to the way I was spreading my legs even farther, trying to grind myself against my heel, the floor, *anything.* He sucked my fingers into his mouth, licking and voracious, and the sensation of his tongue flicking across my fingertips was enough to drive me mad.

He removed them from his mouth but kept them pressed against his lips. "In my heaven, Ivy," he said, "there is no food to eat, but only your pussy. When I taste you, I know that I've tasted salvation. Now place your hands on my knees. You are not allowed to touch yourself under any circumstances."

"*Please,*" I croaked. "Mr. Markham, please."

"*Shh.* Quiet. Watch."

He took the dress and wrapped the soft fabric around himself. "This is where your tits were, Ivy. Where they were rubbing against the dress. Do you know that the night you came here, after we spoke, I came to this very room, to this very chair, and pulled out my cock? It was already hard—it had been hard from the moment I held your wrist in my hand and felt the delicate skin there. I could feel your pulse, your very lifeblood, so close to the surface as I held you." His hand moved slowly up and down his shaft, rubbing the cotton against himself. The wide crest of his crown appeared and disappeared, and damn *how I wanted it inside me.*

"I couldn't wait to get undressed or even take off my shoes. I unbuttoned my trousers only enough to free my dick and then I worked myself harder and faster than I have since I was a schoolboy. I wanted one of your dresses then to climax in. I wanted you to watch as I did it."

His hand moved faster now, and I could hear the fabric rustling as it brushed against the chair and the wool of his pants. "I had to settle for my hand, of course, watching cum spill over onto my fingers and onto my waistcoat when I knew, even then, that it belonged in your cunt, on your tits, in your hair."

My fingers were gripping his thighs so hard that I knew they'd leave marks. I also knew that he liked it, he liked it when I repaid his dominance with fierceness, when I submitted but with teeth and scratching and twisting.

"Watch now," he said. "I'm going to come on this dress. I'm going to mark it. Destroy it. Because you are mine now. You wear the dresses I give you. You climax when I say you can." His breath was ragged now, rough like unpolished granite, rough and lovely. "Say it," he said. "Say that you're mine."

"I'm yours," I breathed. "My body belongs to you. My pleasure belongs to you. Only you."

His other hand caught my face once again. "Only me."

"Only you, but please, I need—" My hands were already sliding off his legs. I couldn't help it. I had to touch myself, *had to*. I was almost weeping with the agony of it.

Effortlessly, he grabbed both my wrists, his long fingers keeping them pinned together at his knee. His eyes glittered green with triumph. "Here it comes," he growled. "Watch."

And watch I did, as ejaculate spurted in thick, white ropes onto what used to be the most expensive dress I owned. He made no noise, his hips stayed still, his hand still a vise around my wrists. But he came hard and long and by the time he was done, my eyes were burning with tears and wet desire was beginning to slide coolly down my thighs.

His cock pulsed one last time and we both watched it together. Then he looked at me, kneeling and trapped, shuddering uncontrollably with the need to be fucked, my dress pooled in his lap and laced with his semen. He looked so powerful, and I was confronted once again with the almost princely virility of him, the raw strength of body and will, and the shudders shook me harder.

He tossed the dress to the side. "You wanted to learn, Ivy. Today, I will teach you the meaning of the word *need*. And it won't be an easy lesson."

He must have seen the horror in my face as I realized that he wasn't going to penetrate me or even bring me off with his fingers or tongue. I started wrestling against his grip then, no plan in mind other than to get my hands free and end this consuming roar of desire. He grinned at my fruitless efforts, and then leaned forward, whispering in my ear, "If you are a good pupil, if I feel satisfied with your progress, then I will reward you."

"Reward me now," I said, my voice strangled. "God, Julian, I can't—"

His mouth slanted against mine, sealing me off from speech and air and thought. He broke off, breath ragged, and when he sat up, I could see that he was getting hard again. "I like it when you call me by my name," he said throatily, and for a moment, I glimpsed that vulnerable, tortured soul that I loved so much, as much as I loved the brusque, dominating mask he wore over it.

He stood and pulled me to my feet. "Come," he said, leading me by my wrists to the door. I felt a flash of apprehension when he opened the door to the hallway—what if a servant saw us? Him pulling me along like a prisoner, me completely naked? But I would be lying if I didn't admit that the thought also incited more lust. I *wanted* other people to know how he owned my body. I wanted the whole world to know. And I wanted the whole world to see how I owned him when he was inside of me, how only I got to see those rare moments of human desperation and vulnerability.

The hallway was empty, and we were inside my room after a short walk. Mr. Markham let me go, with a glance of warning at my hands, and then began searching for a new dress. After he'd selected a dress, a fresh corset, and all of the other assorted underthings, he laid them on the bed. I moved to pick them up, but he stopped me with a hand on my bare stomach.

"I will dress you," he said. "We're taking a bit of a journey and I want you attired in a certain way."

"We're going somewhere?" No. That couldn't be. I couldn't go anywhere like this, certainly not somewhere public . . .

"We have errands to run in York," he said. "You must be fitted for a wedding gown, and I have arrangements to make with my bankers for our honeymoon."

"Dress? Honeymoon?" These things had slipped my mind this morning; everything had slipped my mind. Everything but the sight of Mr. Markham stroking his cock.

"You haven't forgotten in such a short time?" he asked, looking diverted. "You are going to be my wife. And I want you to have the best of everything I can give you—a gleaming wedding dress, a tour abroad that never has to end if you don't want it to."

The idea of marrying Mr. Markham still thrilled me, excited me, but I didn't care about dresses or travels. "I don't want you to buy me things," I said. "I want you to fuck me."

He laughed, clearly delighted by this.

I was not as amused as he was. "We agreed that I wasn't to be your whore. Why do you insist on getting me things I don't want?"

"Because you are mine and it is in my power to give you things. It makes me happy. Will you consent to this, for the sake of my happiness?" He leaned his forehead against mine. "Do it for me, Ivy. Because I am completely at your mercy. My happiness, my fulfillment, my soul, it is all yours to make or destroy."

He brushed his lips against mine, and I couldn't help it—I tried to rub myself against his leg, whimpering when he pulled away. "Julian, I'm begging you," I gasped. "If you must take me to York, fuck me first. Otherwise, it will be unbearable."

"You only think it's unbearable. Imagine what suffering it

will be for me to restrain myself. Now, hold out your leg, it's time for us to dress."

I refused, tucking one ankle behind the other. His eyes glittered and suddenly his hand was sliding down my stomach, his fingers finding my clit.

I moaned, melting against him, my legs falling open as the sensation of him caressing my bud overwhelmed me.

And then he stopped, smug.

"Why?" I asked, my voice dangerously high-pitched.

He lowered his lips to my mouth. "Because when you're coming later tonight, screaming so loudly all of York will be able to hear, it will be worth it. Now hold out your leg."

I did. He expertly slid one stocking up my leg, then the other, making sure to brush the back of his hand against my center as he did. Then came the chemise and the corset: each nipple rolled and plucked into tight furls before he imprisoned them inside. He skipped the drawers and two of the petticoats, which would leave only a single layer in between my legs and the silk of my skirt.

"People will be able to see the outline of my legs," I protested.

"Good," he said.

He expertly slid the dress over my head and shoulders and began tying back the skirt. When he finished, he stepped back to examine me with a critical eye.

"You're stunning," he said. "Simply stunning." He moved forward and pressed his lips to my neck, to my collarbone, pressing his thigh against my pelvis and making me moan. I could feel his hardness pressing into my hip, and it made me feel slightly better about my aching pussy. He was aching too, and that was some comfort.

"I'm going to have Gareth bring the carriage around," he said against my jaw. "Be ready when I call for you. I have a feeling I'm going to need you to suck me off at least once on the ride there."

At least, it *had been* some comfort.

He stepped out the door, then turned. "And pet?"

"Yes?"

"I will know if you've touched yourself. Don't."

I closed my eyes with frustration, but I nodded after a minute.

Fine. *Fine.*

I stomped around my room for a couple moments after he left, gathering up some odds and ends for our sudden trip—hair combs, a spare set of gloves, a small copy of *Rob Roy* that I'd been reading at night. I could barely process that we were going to York—everything was a faded blur next to my need to be satisfied. I yanked my purse off the vanity, swearing under my breath when I knocked the hair comb and brush onto the floor.

It was when I knelt to retrieve them that I saw it—a jagged scratch in the silk wallpaper that extended from beyond the vanity by about an inch. It was thin and barely noticeable unless you were close to the wall, as I was now. I squinted at it, curious. It was not only thin, but straight too—not the crack of plaster settling, not an accidental gouge from moving furniture. I gave the vanity an experimental tug and succeeded in pulling it away from the wall enough to see how the scratch extended into a series of scratches, long and connected. It was a word. No—two words.

Help me.

I moved back, my heart thudding no longer from lust but from fear. *Help me.*

Who had written this? And why? And when?

"She did it, you know. Not long before she died."

I started, adrenaline sluicing through me, turning to see Brightmore framed in the doorway like a malevolent ghost.

"Mrs. Brightmore, you frightened me—"

"She slept in here most nights," Brightmore continued, as if I hadn't spoken. "Like she was afraid of the master. I caught her carving this into the wall with a hatpin one night." Her nostrils flared. "Awful trash. How dare she touch this house? She wasn't even fit to step foot in it."

I had come to terms with Violet's unpopularity—had sometimes felt the same way about her myself—but Brightmore's naked hatred and jealousy of my relative irked me. Still, I wanted answers more than I wanted to defend Violet at that moment, so I swallowed my anger and asked, "Do you know why she would carve something like that?"

"She was deranged," the housekeeper said coldly. "How should I know why someone like that would do what she did?"

"She wasn't deranged," I said, more to myself than to Brightmore. Violet had been many things—tempestuous and difficult included—but not that.

"She couldn't face Mr. Markham," Brightmore said abruptly, taking a step toward me. "She couldn't accept him. She couldn't understand him. And I cleaned up his messes as I always do." She was very close to me now; my neck prickled. "I have to take care of him, because no one else truly can."

I hated the idea that she and Mr. Markham had any sort of relationship at all. I resolved to ask him about it later. But it was the subtext of her words that disturbed me. I kept my voice collected. "What did you do?"

She narrowed her eyes at me. And then she made a noise between a hiss and a scoff, a noise that said *you are not worthy to know*. "I didn't kill her, if that's what you're asking. But I told the master how to handle a wayward wife. And he did."

"Miss Ivy, the carriage—" Gareth's voice was sunny as he came into the room, but he froze as he took in the two of us, mere feet apart, hatred heating the air. He quickly recovered. "Um, the carriage is ready. Mr. Markham took the liberty of packing you a trunk last night and it is already loaded, but I'll be happy to carry out anything else that you need."

Brightmore glared at him, but Gareth refused to leave. He stood resolutely inside the room until she finally swept away, leaving her dark words to fester in my mind along with the scratches behind the vanity.

Help me.

I stared at the marks a moment more, then made to push the table back against the wall. Gareth came over to help me, then straightened as he saw the words.

"What is that?" he asked, his voice strange. "Did you . . . ?"

I shook my head. "Brightmore said it was Violet. She caught her doing it."

Gareth's knuckles were white around the edges of the table, and I remembered the rumors. Poor Gareth. I shouldn't feel sympathy for the man who'd been entangled in my cousin's adultery—especially since I was about to wed the husband who'd been hurt by it. But I did, because in that moment, I saw an entire sea of grief pooling in Gareth's eyes.

"I didn't know she was that unhappy," he said, pushing the vanity back and then going back to the door. He kept his face from me.

"I thought it was common knowledge that she was unhappy with Mr. Markham."

"I think maybe this was about something else," Gareth said, but he offered no explanation for his cryptic analysis and refused to talk anymore as he ushered me down to the courtyard.

CHAPTER 3

*M*r. Markham had indeed arranged for a small trunk to be packed with enough effects to last me for a few days, and also procured refreshments for the hours-long journey, and then we were off. The minute the wheels left the paving stones of the drive and hit the smooth dirt track to Stokeleigh, Mr. Markham drew the shades and beckoned me over.

I moved to the seat next to him, keeping us at a distance for the time being. Just sitting next to him revived the need he'd so carefully stoked this morning, and I needed my head to clear for a few moments at least.

"May I ask you something?"

"Anything, pet," he said fondly.

"How close are you to your housekeeper?" I tried to hide the jealousy in my tone and failed.

He blinked and I could see that my question had been the last thing in the world he'd expected to hear.

"My *housekeeper*?"

"Mrs. Brightmore."

"Yes, I know who my housekeeper is. But you are asking . . . what are you asking again?"

I opened my mouth and then shut it. It wasn't done to ask these kind of things, surely, and I wasn't as naive as everybody thought I was. I knew what men did with their servants, and I knew that most men didn't think it was the place of women to question what they did behind closed doors.

But I also couldn't stomach the not knowing, and etiquette be damned, if I was to marry this man, I didn't want him sharing anything with that dragon. "Are you friends? Do you share your problems with her? Have you fucked her?"

His laugh rumbled through the carriage. "Have I fucked *Brightmore*? God, no." He laughed again. "You cannot be jealous of her, Ivy. Honestly."

"She said that only she could take care of you," I said, a bit stubbornly, not ready to give up.

"Only *you* take care of me." He took my hand and pressed it to his erection. "See?"

I removed my hand. "But she's known you so much longer than I have."

He sighed. "What does that signify? I've spent more time with you in the last week than I've spent with her in the last ten years."

"But you hand-selected her from another house . . . "

Another sigh. "To be honest, I felt responsible for her fate. She had worked in Arabella's home before Arabella married me. Arabella's parents—the Whitefields—died not long after, leaving no heirs. They eventually found a seventh or eighth cousin to inherit the estate, but he sold off the house and the lands, and all the servants were dismissed. When I saw Brightmore working as a maid while I was a guest at another house, I felt it was my duty to give her a better situation. In a way, she had been part of my family and my duty, for however brief a time."

"Oh." That was understandable. Admirable even. I had witnessed firsthand what happened to servants after a family disintegrated. After Thomas had died and my house was auctioned off, the old gardener and his daughter—the only servants who had stayed until the end—were summarily evicted without notice. And I had been powerless to help. Fortunately, they'd found another situation nearby, but that was a rare and lucky thing.

"Don't listen to her, wildcat," Mr. Markham said. "I don't. She didn't want me to hire Gareth, even though he had excellent references and has since been the best valet I've ever had. I ignored her then, as you should now."

I shook my head, anxious to get my final worry out of my head and into the open air. "But you listened once. She said that she helped you with Violet. That she helped you take care of your 'wayward wife.' Mr. Markham, what did she mean by that?"

His face had frozen mid-smile, mid-word, and I could see the way his pupils contracted ever so slightly, as if he were withdrawing into himself. When he finally spoke, his jaw was tight. "I've never taken my housekeeper into my confidence. If you are worried that she and I are close confidants, then please stop. I haven't shared a single detail of my personal life with her since I hired her. But housekeepers know things, Ivy. They can't not know things. And she knew the state of my marriage with Violet. So yes, there was a time when she approached me with her advice, and to my deep regret, I admit that I took it."

I couldn't suppress the fear hovering at the edges of my mind, but he read me, as he always did, and he leaned forward to peer into my eyes. "Precious wildcat," he whispered. "Quiet your jealousy, quiet your fear. You are safe with me. You are loved with me."

And then he effortlessly moved me on top of his lap, hitching up my skirts until my waist was surrounded by silk and my bare sex was flat against his trousers. Despite everything—the scratched-out words and Brightmore and his admission that he had once heeded her directions regarding his marriage—despite all that, heat flared in my core. He buried his face in my neck, nipping and sucking at every available inch of skin, his teeth a delicate torture along my collarbone.

Once again, I couldn't help myself; I started grinding against him, feeling his stiff length under the fabric.

He looked down. "I wish you could see what I see," he said in a low voice. "Your pussy moving against me, so desperate. So needy."

I rubbed harder and faster, feeling the tension building inside me, twining and twining until I thought every muscle and nerve would snap. I threw my head back, feeling it surging—only to have Mr. Markham grab me by the hips and hold me up. Empty air rushed between him and me, cool and unforgiving, and I writhed in his grasp, trying to force myself down.

"Let me come," I pleaded, our conversation now completely gone from my mind.

He grinned. "Absolutely not."

"Please!"

He held me there, mercilessly, cruelly, until several minutes had passed and my body began to unwind. But my cunt pulsed more than ever, heavy between my legs, and my nipples beaded painfully under my corset.

"How do you feel?" he asked.

"Terrible," I told him bluntly.

He laughed.

"It's not funny," I said, a little miffed and more than a little agonized. "I don't think this game is fun at all."

His face turned serious. "This isn't a game, Ivy. It's supposed to be more than fun."

"I thought—"

"You and me, we are more than playmates," he said, one hand letting go of me. He unfastened his trousers, exposing his erection. My body pulsed in response, every cell straining to touch him. He took himself in hand and began rubbing the head of his cock against my sex. I gasped at the feel. He was like steel sheathed in satin—silky maleness, hard and wide.

I began to wriggle against him, urgent to impale myself on that sublime organ, and to my surprise, he let me. He let me notch the head of his cock into my pussy and he held himself upright as I slid down, crying out with bliss as I did. I finally sank to the root, my clit pressed against him, but again his hands were on my hips, buried in the silk skirts, keeping me from moving.

But a muscle in his jaw ticked, and I could see that it took an enormous amount of restraint on his part to keep me from riding him.

"We are more than playmates," he repeated. "What do you feel when I'm inside you?"

"Like I want you to fuck me until I'm beyond my senses."

A faint smile. "Think harder than that. Probe your feelings further."

I wanted to weep with the need to move. He stretched me, filled me, and my whole body sang for him, but it wasn't enough. "I feel . . . full. Complete. But I want more. More of you, like no matter what we do, we'll never be close enough."

His voice was husky. "Keep going."

I could barely catch my breath, my need for friction was so strong. "I feel like you and I are one person, one soul split into two bodies, and when we're joined, it almost feels like that spirit is whole again."

"*Yes*," he told me. "We were meant to be together. You were born to be Ivy Markham. I was born to love you. When I'm deep inside you, I feel my heart beat in tandem with yours. Can you feel it?"

I could. I could feel my body keening for him, canting toward him, as if he were the only warmth in a frozen land. The only music in a soundless void. And when our bodies were connected—

"Yes," I breathed. "I feel it."

"So when I tease you, when I deprive you, all I'm doing is reminding your body—your soul—that it needs mine. And as you yearn, you will know that I am being reminded too. That even when we are not joined, we still are connected, on a deeper level." His mouth softened, warmth suffusing the lines of his face. "Do you understand now?"

I nodded, my throat suddenly tight. I blinked and a single tear traced down my cheek. He leaned forward—shifting himself deliciously inside me—and kissed it.

"Is this a tear of joy?" he asked quietly.

"It is," I said, more tears falling fast now. "I love you."

"And I love you." He reached for something in his jacket pocket and extracted it. It glittered in the faint light of the carriage.

A ring.

"I was so eager to claim you last night that I forgot the most important thing." He slid the ring onto my finger. "There. Now everybody will know that you're mine."

I examined the ring closely, feeling more tears swell as I did. A rose gold band sprouted into two delicate leaves, which held a sizable diamond in place. It winked and shimmered and added a heady weight to my hand. "It's beautiful," I managed.

He looked at me closely. "It was my mother's. Do you like it? We can buy you a new one—"

"No," I interrupted. "It's perfect." And it was. It could have been a band of iron and I still would have loved it, because it came from him. Because someone loved me enough to marry me, despite my poverty, despite my fallen family. After my brother's death, I had given up all hope of ever making a decent match. And here I was, marrying into a family wealthier and more ancient than even my parents would have ever hoped for me.

"Good," he said. "You need to like it. I expect it on your finger at all times—especially when we are in public." He moved again, and I was reminded of our position, of him sunk to the hilt, of me desperate for more. I rocked into him, the engagement ring sending prisms of light cascading around us, yellows and blues and greens darting around our moving bodies.

"Let's marry now," I said. "Today." My voice was tight—I was so close to coming—

He lifted me off himself, groaning as he did, and then I was put on my knees. "Believe me, wildcat, I would like nothing more. But you deserve the best. And the best takes time." He wove his hands through my hair. "Now lick me until I come."

He didn't let me orgasm during our ride, but I was able to bear it better, knowing that this exercise between us was something deeper than the parlor games his friends played. I felt it in my marrow, our connection, as we jostled and rolled our way to York, and I knew that I would never see my hunger for him in the same way. This all-consuming passion we felt for each other was almost spiritual, almost holy, and it went far beyond the mechanical needs and rote fumblings of other people.

Over and over again, Mr. Markham told me how much he loved me, how much his mind craved my mind, how he loved to hear me talk and how he loved to watch me roam outside like a forest sprite. He made me spread my legs, and then he knelt before me, kissing me with fluttering, light kisses until I squirmed in torture. And he told me he couldn't live without me, that we would never spend a night apart so long as we both lived.

I was panting and flushed as the medieval buildings of York began to cut crepuscular shadows through the windows, and by the time we reached our hotel, I was grateful for the oncoming night, which hid my tousled hair and shallow breathing.

The porter brought in our trunks while Mr. Markham arranged for our rooms and for a girl to attend to me, which I protested, but he insisted. "My future wife would have a lady's maid. And truthfully, I should have seen to it the moment you arrived at Markham Hall. I'm not used to thinking about other people's needs. But I will take special care to tend to yours."

And then he flashed a grin, wide and wolfish, and I realized he was very much referencing the need that raged low in my belly.

I put my hand on his arm, feeling shaky and desperate. "How long until we are in our rooms?" I asked. "I can't be in public like this."

He raised an eyebrow. "Why not?"

"*Because*—" My voice was carelessly loud and the porter glanced over at me. "Because," I said again, much lower, "all I can think about is coming. And I'm beginning not to care how or where that happens. I could right now, do you understand? Right here in this hotel lobby."

He smiled again, but this time he bit his lip in a way that made more heat surge within me, like he was trying to stop himself from taking me right then and there.

"Julian?"

I turned, seeing a tall man with a striking face and even more striking blue eyes. He had carved cheekbones and curved lips, with smile lines etched around his eyes and mouth. He'd cut his dark hair short in the week since I'd seen him, and he was in expensive evening wear rather than the more casual clothes I'd seen on him before, but I'd still recognize Silas Cecil-Coke anywhere.

"Silas," Mr. Markham said, extending a hand, stepping out of our intense exchange as smoothly as a person steps from a hansom cab. Silas ignored the proffered hand and gave Mr. Markham a back-clapping hug instead. I saw Mr. Markham tense a little—he was not the kind of personality that invited such brotherly embraces—but his expression was easy enough as the man pulled back. "I thought you were in London with the others."

Silas gave a one-shouldered shrug. "My elder brother managed to produce another one of those squishy pink things to add to the pile already at Coke Manor. I came up to give the requisite *oohs* and *ahs* to the latest usurper standing between me and the bulk of my inheritance." And then the inevitable grin emerged, bright and sunny. "Damned cute usurper, if I may say so. A little man this time. They named him Silas, after me." I could tell, despite his deprecation, that he was actually quite the adoring uncle.

"But enough about me. What are you doing in York, you devil? We couldn't pry you out of Markham Hall last week and now here you are gallivanting about town without us."

Mr. Markham took my hand. The gesture wasn't about power or teaching or anything other than the simple desire to show someone close to him that we were linked, together. "I've made an offer of marriage to Ivy and she's accepted. We've come to make some further arrangements."

Silas turned toward me, and I knew the signs of our ride here were as apparent as if they'd been written on my face. My rumpled hair and clothes, my parted and swollen lips, my dilated pupils. I was almost frantic with the need to relieve the hours of pent-up tension, and my mind was beginning to stray to shameful places, and I couldn't stop myself from taking in Silas's physique—more slender than Mr. Markham's, but still robust enough in the shoulders and arms to suggest an active lifestyle—and then to imagine him fucking me. Him *and* Mr. Markham fucking me at the same time.

Oh God. I had to get upstairs.

Silas took my hand and brushed his lips against the back of it, and even this small amount of contact was enough to make my eyes flutter closed. His grip tightened on my fingers. "Miss Leavold," he said, his voice sonorous and smooth. "Let me offer my congratulations."

"Thank you," I said, barely able to utter the words. My mind was slowly shutting down, it seemed, shedding one layer of civilization and etiquette after another.

"We have only just arrived after our journey," Mr. Markham said, watching Silas's fingers wrapped around my own.

Silas let go—reluctantly it seemed—and straightened his jacket. Then he smiled, his mouth curving into an upside-down triangle of mirth. "So Julian Markham is taking the yoke once again. You'll have your hands full with Julian, let me tell you. Coke Manor was only a few miles away from Markham Hall, and the things we got up to as boys, and then at Eton and at Oxford . . . "

"I'm sure I've already seen the worst of him," I said, mustering a glare at my fiancé. "I'm confident the future can't contain any worse."

And then there was a lull, where a flash of clear-thinking sent the boxes in the back of my mind singing and shouting again, where perhaps all three of us were remembering what had actually been claimed of Julian Markham's worst behavior.

"Let's dine together," Silas suggested, smoothing over the pause. "This hotel has a fine restaurant, and their wine cellar is very good."

I shot a look at Mr. Markham. No, we could not accept a dinner invitation, not when he had promised me relief tonight, and it was already late—

"Well, we only just arrived and need to change," Mr. Markham said.

I breathed a sigh of relief.

Mr. Markham met my eyes. "But we'd be happy to join you."

"Marvelous! I shall procure us a table and a good bottle."

"Then we shall see you shortly."

No! I watched this arrangement with horror, and I opened my mouth to register my protests, but I was already being swept past Silas and up the stairs. "You seem agitated," Mr. Markham murmured in my ear. "Now why could that be?"

We were up the stairs now, and the porter was holding open the door to a room, as a woman swathed in black silk came at us from the end of the corridor. "Miss Leavold, your room is here," she informed me. She gave Mr. Markham's hand, wrapped securely around my waist, a look that told me she knew exactly the kind of intimacies we shared and that she saw things like this often and was too jaded to care.

Mr. Markham kissed my cheek and said into my ear, "I'll be with you in just a moment. And again—I'll know if you touch yourself while I'm gone."

With that warning, I was herded into the room by the hotel matron, who ensured that everything was to my satisfaction and then left. I couldn't sit, I couldn't stand still, so I paced, praying that Mr. Markham would end my suffering before we went down to dinner.

The door opened after a minute or two, and he came in.

I was on him at once. "Please," I begged. "Please."

He slid his arms around my waist. "I'm tempted," he said. "But to see you so undone at dinner . . . that's a temptation too."

"But Silas . . . " I said, and then I shivered, because I felt his fingers working on my dress buttons.

He walked around me, untying my skirt and bustle, and then the dress fell away. "But that is *even more* tempting," he said. "I want Silas to see how beautiful you are like this. I want him to want you and then know that you are indelibly mine."

He walked over to my trunk, opening it and pulling out a fresh frock, this one a wine-colored silk with a low neckline and large bustle.

"Julian, no," I said, seeing that he was about to dress me, not about to fuck me. "No, no, no—"

The dress whispered over my head, Mr. Markham deftly affixing it closed, and then attending to the bustle and the sprays of black lace that frothed at the neckline and at the cap sleeves. I felt a surge of anger then—real anger, limb-shaking anger—and I slapped him hard across the cheek, a crack that resounded through the room.

He growled and crushed his lips to mine, and the press of his body against my own left no doubt what state my rebellion had brought him to. My body responded immediately, the anger fueling my lust, and I seized him, digging my fingers into his dinner jacket, grinding my pelvis against his erection, determined to end this torture right now.

And then his hand was on my neck, the pads of his fingers just barely denting the yielding skin and tendons. "Kneel, Ivy."

"No," I said, and it was more like a cat's hiss than speech, and his nostrils flared.

"For that, you don't get to touch me," he said. "And the next time I have to ask, I'm taking you over my knee."

He must have seen the thought that crossed my mind at this, because he added, "And I won't let you come. In fact, I won't let you climax until tomorrow night. And believe me, I'll be watching you like a hawk through all the long hours of your denial."

It was that threat that punctured my little insurrection. I felt the fight leave my body, my poor, neglected body, and I sank to the floor.

"Let me touch you at least," I pleaded.

"No," and his face was almost cruel as he pulled himself out. "No, you may not touch me. Put your hands behind your back."

I was starting to cry again. I felt raw, flayed open with desire, and I hated it. Except I didn't. Part of me trusted Mr. Markham, trusted that this was something that would feel all the more stunning for the work it took to get there. Part of me lapped up the suffering and the misery, because it was the man I loved giving it to me, and because I knew it was torment for him too, to not make love to me, to not give me what I wanted.

And I *had* asked for all of this, after all.

He fisted his cock and began to rub himself. It was hard and fast—not the leisurely way he'd done it this morning. It was as if this truly were a punishment for me, something to be doled out, not something to be enjoyed. "When we go downstairs to dine," he said, his face and voice betraying nothing of his activity, "I expect you to be completely obedient. No matter what I ask you to do. Understood?"

I nodded, mute with want, unable to tear my eyes away from the erotic sight of Mr. Markham pleasuring himself, of the way his longer fingers circled the thick, veined shaft, almost vicious-looking and brutal in their grip.

"If you trust me, if you behave, then our lesson in needing can end and I will reward you." He saw which way my gaze tended. "Is this what you want, Ivy?" he jerked his head toward his erection. "Is this what you want inside of you?"

"God, *yes*," I cried. "I don't care if you want to fuck me in front of all the guests at this hotel, just take me already!"

His mouth twitched, and his dick pulsed, and then he grabbed the skirt of my dress, finishing with four or five long pulls, his seed jetting onto the claret silk.

Another dress ruined, I thought, but I couldn't bring myself to care about the fabric just then. I only cared that I had been marked once again, claimed, and that while the draped folds of the skirt would mostly hide the stain, I would still know it was there for anyone to see if they looked.

"I'll be inside you later tonight," he promised. "And it won't be quick."

He calmly readjusted himself and his clothing, and like that, it was as if nothing had happened. "Fix your hair, pet," he said. "We're already late."

* * *

TEN MINUTES LATER, and we were walking arm in arm down the main staircase. Right before we had left my room, he had me spread my legs and brace my hands on the vanity table. My skirt and petticoat were hiked up to my waist, and then he was kneeling behind me, parting my folds with his tongue.

"Just to make sure you're still ready for the final part of our lesson," he'd said, and then he'd stoked me to further flame, sucking and licking, his strong hands parting the cheeks of my ass to give him better access. He'd stopped at the very moment of no return, as if he knew my body better than I did, and stood.

"Skirts down, Miss Leavold. It's time for dinner."

And what else could I do? I lowered the silks, feeling like his whore, and hating how much I loved it. As we walked, I could still feel the memory of his tongue between my legs. It was agony.

"I've no doubt that Silas would like to play with you tonight," Mr. Markham said as we walked down. "He could barely tear his eyes away from you in the lobby."

"Oh," I said, and it was an oh of *yes please, please, please*, and another memory pushed through my mind, the feeling of Silas's erection in my hands, of how long and hot and stiff it had been.

Mr. Markham stopped before we reached the dining room and took a stray tendril of my hair between his fingers. "He is invited to help me please you. But," and here he stopped and faced me entirely, "you have the final say on Silas. I want him to touch you and sample you because it gets me hard knowing how much you arouse my friends. I think he would make you feel good—he is very skilled. But you are my own, my own wildcat, and if you only want me to touch you, I understand."

I flushed with the small thread of shame that stitched through me, but I was beyond shame at this point anyway, and so I admitted, "I would like him to touch me." A shuddering breath, and then, "Julian, right now I want *everyone* to touch me. The things I'm thinking about right now—"

"I know, wildcat. And it delights me to know that I have made you like this. And," he gave me a sudden kiss, his tongue moving against mine, stroking deep into my mouth, "whenever you call me Julian, I get hard. Feel."

I did, the briefest of movements, since we were, after all, in a busy hotel in one of the largest cities in England. He was indeed hard again, hard as steel. "Ah," he hissed as my hand brushed by him. "Squeeze it. Squeeze it like you hate me."

I did, loving how powerful I felt at that moment, making him as inflamed as I was. He sucked in a breath.

"I love you," he said and then he took me roughly by the elbow and guided me into the dining room, where Silas—and I hoped my release—awaited.

CHAPTER 4

*S*ilas had secured us a private booth near the back of the restaurant, a rich leather affair scooped out of the wall and separated from the other diners by red curtains, which were currently tied back. Mr. Markham gestured for me to slide in first and then he followed, which left me sandwiched between the two men. The warmth from their hips and thighs suffused my skin through my dress, and I couldn't help the shudder that passed through me when Silas turned to speak and his arm brushed against my own. I kept my eyes down, afraid to meet Silas's or Mr. Markham's gaze, afraid that the slightest stimulation would send me whirling out of control.

Glasses of wine were set before us, the waiter came to inform us of our dinner choices—Mr. Markham ordered for me—and I stared at the tablecloth throughout it all, vaguely knowing that it wouldn't be proper for me to be panting and squirming at the table, but also knowing that I was beyond caring.

Mr. Markham's hand whispered along the back of my neck. "Ivy has been a very obedient girl today," he murmured. "*Very* obedient."

"Is that so?" Silas asked, and I could tell by the tenor of his voice that he immediately took Mr. Markham's meaning.

"Tell him, wildcat. Tell him about your day."

I could not. Words were obscure, foggy things that seemed unimportant, and my hands and legs were trembling; the same tremors were vibrating through my chest and making it impossible to breathe or think normally. All I could think of was unfastening Mr. Markham's pants—or Silas's, I was starting not to care about the particulars—and then of mounting one of them, right here in the booth.

Silas laughed. "It must have been quite a day, Miss Leavold. You seem speechless. And I can see the flush creeping up your neck now, as if you were burning up inside. Shall I check and see?"

I could only look at him, my lips parted, and then his hand stole over my knee under the table, pulling slowly at my dress. Fabric collected in my lap and my legs felt dangerously exposed to the world, even though I knew the floor-length tablecloth hid everything from view, including Silas's hand, which now slid against my inner thigh. I held my breath, wanting him to go farther but also unsure of Mr. Markham's reaction.

Mr. Markham continued to touch the back of my neck, playing with the small curls at my nape, watching the drama under the table unfold. "Spread your legs for Silas," he said, and I did. I spread them as wide as I could, suddenly desperate for Silas, desperate for him to use his fingers, tongue, cock, anything so long as it ended in me climaxing.

His fingers skated past the edge of my stocking and then they were dancing across my center, over and over again. "So wet," Silas said quietly. "So swollen." And one finger parted the petals of my pussy, just barely, just enough that he could lift his finger to his mouth and taste me.

"How does she taste?" Mr. Markham asked.

Silas smiled. "Perfect." His finger returned, this time delving further in, and I pushed myself against it, wanting him to stop teasing and actually touch me.

"How long did you deny her, Julian?"

"Only since this morning."

"She's so responsive," Silas said wonderingly, watching my face as he ran his thumb over my clit. I was actively rocking against his hand now, my hands gripping the table to keep my upper body stable, so that our tableau betrayed nothing to our fellow diners.

"You have no idea," Mr. Markham said. "You should see her in bed."

"I would very much like to," he said. I could now clearly see the hard ridge straining his trousers, a ridge which he was casually rubbing with his other hand. The sight of it was unbearably erotic; Mr. Markham was right. There was something so powerful in seeing how I affected other men, in seeing how badly they wanted me and feeling Mr. Markham's possessive touch on me all the while.

As if responding to my thoughts, Mr. Markham's arm moved between the back of the booth and my waist, and then his other hand joined Silas's, caressing my cunt with soft strokes. Their fingers moved in between and around each other's, sometimes wrestling for access to my clit, sometimes sliding into me together.

I looked down and then I knew it was all but over. Black tailcoat sleeves. Starched white cuffs. Glittering silver cufflinks. And those separate male hands fucking my cunt with reverent relentlessness.

"I—" It came out as a breathy moan, and dimly I remembered that I should be quiet, I should be still, but there was a thumb circling my clit and a finger sliding knuckle-deep into my backside, and then nothing else could possibly exist.

"You what?" Mr. Markham asked.

"I'm going to come," I managed, trying to make it sound like a warning, but failing because the neediness in my voice betrayed me.

"That's the idea, darling," Silas said. "If it wouldn't have us arrested, I'd pull you onto this table and fuck you as you did."

"No fucking, Silas," Mr. Markham said.

"Fine," his friend sighed. "Then I suppose I would have to watch as Markham fucked you. A shame. You have such a deliciously tight pussy, Miss Leavold. I would love to feel it hot and quivering around my cock."

It was too much. The sight of them working me—half in tandem, half in competition—their faces casual and placid as they brought me off under the table, the sweet pressure in all the right places . . . not to mention the entire day hitherto this, of being teased and denied so many times . . . my hips were rocking even harder now as I tried to ride their hands. My fingers were white from gripping the table edge, and I could feel my breasts swell painfully under my corset. It was coming, that initial wave that would drive me to frenzy, and drive me to frenzy it did, cinching every already tense muscle into a knot of raw physical lust.

"Harder," I moaned, my head falling back. "Deeper. More, please, I need more." I didn't care how loud I was or how obvious my pleasure was anymore. I only needed those fingers to keep doing what they were doing—and then another finger slid into my ass and the circling against my clit redoubled—and then there it was, the peak, the height, and I cried out, my womb knotting and then exploding, sending white lights dancing around the edges of my vision, sending convulsions tearing through my body. They came and came and came, as the two gentlemen in dinner jackets buried their fingers in my pussy right there in the restaurant, and I heard Silas mutter, "Christ," as my channel kept squeezing his fingers, the waves cresting and crashing and cresting again.

"Oh," I breathed, "*oh*," and the convulsions slowly turned into quiet little spasms spaced far apart, until I was slumped against Mr. Markham, feeling drained and weak.

I heard Mr. Markham's voice rumble through his chest, and then the waiter's voice, and then Silas's.

"She's had a fit. The heat, I think, and the exhaustion of the journey. We must see her to her rooms."

"Of course, sir. Shall I send for the physician?"

"Not yet, but have the staff stay alert for our word," Silas said, completely seriously. "She may revive yet, but I won't take any chances."

Relief swept through me as I heard the table being dragged away—Mr. Markham quickly tugging down my skirt before it did—and then as I felt myself being lifted into his arms, like I really had fainted. I heard the other diners murmuring around us as we walked out, but I kept my eyes closed and limbs limp. Not hard, considering I barely had the energy to move.

"Did you see the looks on their faces?" Silas asked, laughing, after we'd been out of the dining room two or three minutes. "That man at the table across from us—I thought he was going to have a fit of his own!"

"You may open your eyes now, Ivy," Mr. Markham said.

I obeyed. We were going up the stairs and his face was close to mine as he carried me. His eyes were soft, loving, and his dark hair was burnished into something lighter in the bright lamp-light of the hotel. He looked like a man from another time, a highwayman or a lost prince, with brilliant glass-green eyes and high cheekbones and a mouth that looked like it wanted nothing more than to devour me.

I closed my eyes again. "I can't believe I did that," I said, waiting for the embarrassment to flood through me. It didn't.

"It was beautiful," Mr. Markham said. "You were beautiful."

"Every man in that restaurant was adjusting himself as we walked out, and I think even some of the women were fanning themselves," Silas added. "The dull ones will buy the story of a fit, but any person who's been properly fucked before will know exactly what they were looking at. And they will love it."

A door opened. We were finally to our room. "Am I invited in?" Silas asked.

Mr. Markham glanced down at me. "Do you need to sleep? Or do you want more?"

I would always want more. When it came to Mr. Markham, I would always *need* more.

"I don't need to sleep," I whispered, and Silas stepped in and closed the door.

MR. MARKHAM EASED me into a chair, then went to ensure that the door was locked. Despite the fierce totality of the climax I'd just had, the fire low in my belly slowly rekindled as I witnessed these two men shrugging off their jackets and unknotting their cravats as they walked toward my chair. Mr. Markham knelt before me, his shirt now open at the throat, showing his rapidly thrumming pulse.

"You are so beautiful," he said, and he gently tugged off my silk heels, kissing each foot as it was freed. "You learned very well today. You learned to trust me with your desire, no matter how far I pushed. It's time for your reward. What would you like?"

I looked down at him as he peered up at me through dark eyelashes, his high forehead tilted back in supplication. He was so virile, so *male*, and seeing him kneeling in front of me sent as much desire spiking through my body as seeing him dominate me. It reminded me that he was more vulnerable than I was, that he was ceding something powerful and precious to me by making me his wife. He might tease me for a few hours out of the day, but his soul was mine to have for the rest of our years.

Perhaps he saw this realization in my eyes, because he laid his head against my knee in a gesture of humility and submission. I stroked through his hair, the thick, dark waves of it, and after a few moments, I used a finger to raise his face up, past my own and to the ceiling.

The long, corded arch of his throat was exposed, and I bent down and kissed it, feeling his restraint and repressed strength as I turned my kiss into a firm, sharp bite. He trembled and his hands twitched around my feet, but he remained still and passive for me, even as the shifting of his hips told me that his arousal was becoming unbearable. I held my teeth there for several seconds, loving the feel of his wild pulse, the smell of sun and greenery that always clung to him.

I pulled away with one last flick of my tongue dancing across his Adam's apple and sat up again, looking down at him like a queen might look down upon a subject.

"Wildcat," he said raggedly, "let me reward you."

Silas had been watching silently this whole time, maintaining a respectful distance as Mr. Markham and I completed our exchange of power, but now he came forward and knelt before me as well. Two pairs of eyes—one pair fern green and the other bright blue—gazed up at me with a heady combination of lust and devotion.

"Undress me," I finally said. "I want to feel you both on my skin."

They both leapt to obey, helping me out of the chair, fingers digging into buttons and ties, and I sighed against the warmth of their movements, sighing again as I was divested of my clothes. Silas nimbly unfastened my corset, and my sighs turned into a sudden intake of breath as the cool air finally tickled against my aching nipples and swollen breasts.

Silas brushed his lips around the swells, kissing in a spiral until his mouth was sucking hot and wet on a furled peak. My back arched and my hand went to Silas's head, holding him fast where he was. I felt and heard his low chuckle at my eagerness, and then he reached down, his hands sliding past the heart shape of my bottom and then hoisting me up so that my legs were around his waist, his mouth affixed to my breast the entire time.

As he walked me over to the bed, I marveled at how different his body felt from Mr. Markham's. Silas was just as tall, just as toned, but there was something urbane and smooth about him, about his entire bearing, as if he charmed his way through life rather than growled through it like Mr. Markham did. Even his hands under my ass felt polished and refined. And as he laved my nipple with his talented tongue, and as I began—more or less unconsciously—grinding my cleft against his stone-hard cock, one got the sense that Silas was never far away from a wide grin or a loud laugh. Joy and mirth—they suffused him, like an affable light.

Mr. Markham was correct earlier today. What Silas did with us, with the others, that was playing, a game for the wealthy and bored to idle away their time. When Mr. Markham and I were alone together, it was something else entirely—something unique and deep and hallowed.

Which wasn't to say that I didn't enjoy the playing.

Silas walked us over to the bed, and my eyes met Mr. Markham's over Silas's shoulder. He had shucked his shirt, so I could see the planes and furrows of his flat stomach and the way his torso tapered into narrow hips, a defined line of muscle making an emphatic *V* leading to his groin.

His eyes moved down, seeing my pelvis flush against Silas's, and his jaw set. In an instant, he was next to us, and there was palpable jealousy in the way he plucked me from his friend's grasp and laid me across the bed. But his stiffness and labored breathing confirmed what he had told me before dinner, that the jealousy was only fuel for his desire, and so I felt no guilt about reaching for both of them and pulling them both down on top of me, both men all muscle and limbs and roving hands.

Mr. Markham's mouth met mine first, a hard kiss that felt more like a branding. His hand cupped the back of my head, and he parted my lips with his own, sliding his tongue against mine, licking past my teeth and deep into my mouth. I was panting when he broke away, heat flushing up my belly and up my neck, and his eyes glittered triumphantly.

Meanwhile, Silas had been tracing circles on the taut skin of my stomach, looping ever wider loops around my navel. "I'd like to follow this blush down to its source, Markham," he said. "That is, if you permit it." There was nothing but brotherly amusement in his voice, as if his friend's jealousy was an adorable quirk that he'd long since grown used to.

Mr. Markham's mouth twitched and a rare smile creased his face. He kissed my neck and then my shoulder. "Am I being selfish with you?" he murmured into my collarbone.

"Yes," I whispered. "And I love it."

Silas pressed his palm to my sternum and then ran his hand down to the swell in between my legs. "He should be selfish with you. You are quite delicious, and the moment the shepherd looks away, you can be guaranteed that a wolf will be there to snatch you up." He lowered his head and dragged his teeth along one nipple to underscore his point. Mr. Markham was kissing my neck now, and once again there were two different hands caressing my folds, drawing lines in the creases where my thighs joined my body.

"But I *promise*," and Silas looked at me with mock solemnity, "that you can trust me not to breach Julian's trust *too* much. At the very least, I won't fight back if he decides to hurl me to the floor in an envious rage."

A quiet laugh rippled through the three of us, and Silas shed the faux-serious face immediately, grinning widely. Mr. Markham lifted his head and our eyes met and I knew that Silas was right. Intrinsic trust was strung between them, and now it was strung between me as well, and tonight would only bring pleasure, not discomfort, to the man Silas and I both loved.

And easily bruised egos be damned, as I kissed Julian, I twined my fingers in Silas's hair and pushed his head down, past my breasts, past my ribs, down to my navel, where he touched his lips to the divot there and began kissing his way to my sex.

For the next several minutes, there was nothing in my world but the two different textures of Silas's and Julian's hair; Julian's mouth on my mouth and on my neck and on my breasts; and Silas's tongue licking at my seam, alternating between sucking at my clit and penetrating my entrance. I could feel the sweat sheening on my body as Silas cleverly manipulated me; all my nerves and sinews tightened and tightened, until everything from my chest to my knees felt like a piano wire about to snap.

But I wasn't ready yet. I wanted them to worship me like this forever, but I also wanted the rigid steel of their cocks, wanted those cocks rubbing against me, sliding against my palms, burying themselves in me.

I let go of Silas's hair to tug at Mr. Markham's pants, which he wriggled easily out of, his large dick springing free as he came back to kiss me. I circled my fingers around him, marveling for the umpteenth time how large he was. He made a low noise of pleasure against my mouth as I continued to stroke him, and his hips were lifting off the bed as he began to fuck my hand.

"I need you inside," I breathed. "Julian—"

Mr. Markham lifted me like I was a doll, and in a second's work, we were both sitting on the edge of the bed, me positioned so that my back was to his chest and I was facing Silas, who sat back on his heels and watched us with my juices still glistening on his lips.

The tip of Mr. Markham's cock was poised at my opening, and with one hand on my hip and the other holding the base of his erection, he slowly guided me down. Inch by inch he stretched me, pushing against my swollen sex, and I was wound so tightly that every incremental movement made me cry out and shudder, which made my lover growl in response.

"Fuck," he muttered, as I finally took him to the root and came to rest against his thighs.

Then Silas was there, and he gently raised one of my legs and hooked it behind Mr. Markham's and then did the same with the other, so that even though I rested on top of Mr. Markham's lap, I was now spread wide open, my calves locked against the outside of his.

Silas knelt, flashing me his amiable grin, and then he pressed his face against my cunt once more. He sucked and nibbled on my bud as Mr. Markham moved underneath me, and then I felt the heat of his tongue moving from my clitoris to the stretched folds around the base of Mr. Markham's cock.

The sensation was too much, and I sank against Mr. Markham's chest, and even he moaned as Silas's ministrations flickered across the place where we were joined. Mr. Markham's hands circled my waist, large and possessive, and he started to move me back and forth. I held on to Silas's head for balance, my fingers gripping his hair for dear life as I felt Mr. Markham inside me, pressing against my womb and then rubbing against that impossible spot lower down, the spot that made my toes curl and my hips buck.

"Come for us, wildcat," Mr. Markham said. "Show us how much you like to be fucked by two adoring men."

The piano wire was about to snap, about to split and lash and fly, and I threw my head back, surrendering to the impending fracture. I held Silas's head tight to me as I began rocking toward my orgasm, using the lovely organ inside and the lovely mouth outside to hurtle myself forward. I became a creature of nothing but raw need, not remembering Silas's name or his wealth or his position as a gentleman, not remembering anything about Julian save that he was *mine*, my own, and we were only need embodied, noise and sweat and heat.

"That's it," Julian coaxed. "Show us, pet. Make that beautiful pussy come."

I came. With Silas's mouth everywhere and with Julian's cock filling me, I came. And I came hard.

It started at my clitoris, a fire and flame that moved like a wave, rolling back and then crashing against my cunt and womb, retracting and then crashing through my hips and thighs, and then finally shaking my entire body, tremors and tingles that raced along every nerve to the tips of my fingers and toes. I heard Mr. Markham swearing as the convulsions squeezed him and I felt Silas's smile against the soft lips of my cunt as he continued to tongue me.

"Julian," I pleaded, as the waves kept coming and coming.

"I'm here, wildcat," he rasped in my ear. "And now it's our turn."

With my pussy still clenching, he lifted me off him, and I whimpered at the abrupt emptiness. I was put on all fours on the bed, with Mr. Markham kneeling behind me and Silas coming up to join us after removing his trousers. He knelt in front of me, his member—no less impressive than Mr. Markham's—jutting out from his lean hips.

Without warning, Mr. Markham plunged into me, sinking to the hilt on the first thrust, and I cried out, the deeper angle bruisingly delicious, turning my already hard nipples into tight jeweled points as Silas slowly stroked himself.

"Ivy," growled Mr. Markham. "Don't you want to thank Silas for making you come?"

I nodded, and then Silas moved closer, the head of his dick only the barest breath away from my lips. He was so polite, hesitant almost, and I got the sudden flash of insight that he wasn't used to taking the reins in the bedchamber like Mr. Markham was. He was so charming and handsome and laid-back, I imagined that most women were more than happy to crawl over him and do all the work. Women like Molly, who liked to take control anyway. If it had been my Julian in front of me, my mouth would have been taken already. But instead Silas waited patiently, one hand gripping himself, the other resting against his thigh.

Mr. Markham was more than willing to take control on his friend's behalf, however. His hand fisted in my hair and yanked my head back. "Open up," he ordered. "Open that pretty mouth and let him slide in. I want you to suck him like he's me, do you understand? Suck his cock like it's mine."

He didn't let go of my hair, and my eyes were watering, but my pussy was wetter than ever, a second climax knotting itself around Julian's ruthless thrusts. I parted my lips and moaned as Silas entered my mouth, the almost apologetic look vanishing from his face, replaced with something more primal. And then his hand was in my hair too, his fingers tangling in the tendrils along with Mr. Markham's, and he began moving his hips to bring himself in and out of me, gasping whenever I flattened my tongue against the underside of his cock.

Behind me, Mr. Markham's other hand dug into my hip, hard and uncaring; his fucking became raw and rough, animal noises tearing from his throat as he rammed into my cunt like a man possessed. Delight and desire flared in my chest; I was the one doing this, I was the one rending the controlled Julian Markham in two. Julian Markham, who barely blinked or panted as he came on my dress, became ferociously undomesticated whenever he sheathed himself inside me, and in turn, it made me wilder, made me feel just as brutal and uncivilized. I spread my legs wider, wanting him deeper, wanting him everywhere.

The two hands in my hair, and the sensation of two cocks pistoning inside me, and the erotic sight of Silas's hips flexing as he fucked my mouth . . . the explosion built in me once more, making me moan and whine around Silas.

"Silas is going to come, Ivy," Julian said, and his voice was so rough, rasping over the sound of our bodies slapping together. "And you are going to take it all. And then you're going to come on my cock and you are going to milk me. Hard."

On cue, Silas swelled in my mouth, his motions growing jerky and uneven, and then with a soft moan, he spilled onto my tongue and down my throat, his hands on either side of my head, holding me still as he spurted. His noises and the delicious feeling of his cock pulsing was enough to send me over the edge on its own, but the moment his orgasm ended, he was on the other side of me next to Mr. Markham, reaching down to fondle my clitoris while Mr. Markham kept hold of my hair and my hip for leverage as he pounded into me.

"Oh God!" I cried, this third orgasm sawing through me with a viciousness unlike anything I had ever felt, and I wasn't sure I could survive it. I was coming to pieces, coming unknit and unmade, and Julian kept fucking and Silas kept rubbing and I was screaming through it all, until, with a loud hiss, Mr. Markham came so hard inside me that I could feel his seed lashing against my walls and feel his cock convulsing. He kept his hand on my hip and kept pounding into me through the duration of his climax, sinking his teeth into my shoulder and growling as he did.

After a few long minutes, his thrusting slowed and his teeth left my skin and my vision finally began to clear. The three of us fell backward on the bed into a tangle of limbs and panting, Mr. Markham still buried inside of me.

"Thank you for sharing yourself with me," Silas said, all gentlemanly politeness, despite the sweat on his forehead and despite the sleepy cock currently pressed against my thigh.

My eyes seemed to close all on their own, and a happy sigh escaped me when Mr. Markham's hand reached around me to cup my breast and Silas laid his head against my shoulder.

"It was my pleasure," I said, and those words had never been truer.

CHAPTER 5

I woke twice that night. The first was to Mr. Markham moving against me, his shaft seeking entrance to my cleft, and I sleepily parted my legs, resting one on his hip as my breasts pressed against his chest. I felt lips on my back—Silas was kissing me there—and for several long minutes, there was nothing but slow dreamy thrusts and the press of Silas's erection against my ass and the sound of skin rasping on fabric. When my orgasm came, it was gentle and sweet, and I was drifting back into sleep even as Mr. Markham shuddered and released into me.

The second time I woke, the floor-length curtains had parted and the blue-black light of early morning limned the window frame and the balcony outside, along with a tall figure. I knew without looking that the man still in bed with me was my own Mr. Markham, but the warmth of the room made the pre-dawn air look cool and attractive, and so in a moment, I was standing next to Silas, wrapped in Mr. Markham's dressing robe.

He'd pulled on his trousers but nothing else, leaving his ridged and slender torso exposed to the open air. He leaned against the railing, surveying the street below, seeming amused by the early morning bustle of food delivery wagons and street vendors and sporadic hansom cabs.

"Too warm?" he asked, not looking at me.

I affirmed that I was and leaned against the railing as well. The world was a different place in the early morning, when the debauched had finally gone to bed and the industrious were barely awake.

"He's in love with you, you know," Silas remarked, still not looking away from the road.

I flushed, wheeling around to make sure Mr. Markham was well asleep and couldn't hear us talking about him. Satisfied that our conversation was not being eavesdropped upon, I turned back to Silas. "I know."

Now he turned and braced his back against the railing, folding his arms across his chest. On any other man, the gesture might have seemed hostile or aggressive, but Silas made it seem friendly. Casual. "Do you really?" he asked.

Defensiveness rippled along my skin like invisible chain mail, but I couldn't refute Silas. It had only been a couple of months, and by any standards, that was too short a time to claim to know someone, however intimately. I barely knew him and I now barely knew myself—I'd always been the girl who had done whatever she wanted, sure, but how could I know that marriage to Mr. Markham wouldn't cage me instead of free me? I wanted to be next to him always . . . but what if the institution of marriage, the boundaries that came with it, the expectations . . . what if they poisoned that love for me?

For the first time, the ring on my finger felt more like a shackle than a promise.

Yes, I wanted to say. I knew that he loved me. But there was so much complication surrounding it all that I couldn't actually find the words.

Silas and I didn't speak for a long moment, staying quiet in the breeze.

"He married his first wife in the York Minster," Silas finally said, nodding his head toward the cathedral towers spiking up above the other buildings. "He loved Arabella, you know. People often think he didn't, because it was arranged between their parents, but he did. He was wrecked after her death." He sighed.

I thought of Arabella, of how Mrs. Harold had accused Mr. Markham of intentionally moving her to a climate that would force her death. I wanted to know more about her, about their marriage. "Did he know her before they married?"

Silas nodded. "Her family was well-known in the county—moneyed and connected—and she was the inevitable match for him from her birth. The right breeding and the right dowry. But they had a genuine connection too. They exchanged letters while he was at Oxford and even while he traveled . . . I think he found something refreshing in her. Something sweet. I would say it was her innocence, but I think it was something slightly different. Rather, I think he felt like she would accept his world-liness, his jadedness, knowingly, and still remain as she was. Much how he feels about you, I suspect."

I glanced back into the dark room, where the long, languid form of Mr. Markham still stretched across the bed.

"But I'm hardly innocent," I said, gesturing between me, Silas, and the bed. "Certainly not in the unspoiled, untouched way that Arabella must have been."

Silas shook his head. "That's not what I mean. I mean that your sense of self—your ability to love and experience and live—can persist, despite proximity to darker things. Some people like Molly, they can get hard. Cynical. They stop trusting and even-tually they stop opening their hearts. They calcify, slowly, into living stone. Your cousin was much the same," Silas said, drawing my thoughts away from Molly. "She was also the oppo-site of Arabella. Passionate and strong, or so she seemed. And in you, I think Julian has finally found everything he was looking for, the synthesis of what he worshipped about Arabella and craved from Violet. The passion and also the ability to remain unsullied by the world."

I should say *thank you*, I should feel flattered. My brain fumbled looking for the appropriate response, all as my heart sank under the weight of this expectation.

I could be Mr. Markham's lover and I could be his wife . . . but could I be his moral anchor? Could I bear the weight of another's heart and mind leaning on mine?

And what if I didn't remain unsullied? What if I grew hard like Molly or Violet? Despite my determination to never see him with Brightmore, I had never deluded myself into thinking Mr. Markham would remain physically loyal to me for our entire marriage—everyone knew that husbands strayed, even those who were less sexually rapacious than my future spouse. But if he did, could I remain unhardened by that? Could I even remain *with* him? I wasn't, after all, bred to endure quietly the way most women were. When things grew painful, my instinct was to flee.

And Silas had mentioned Violet, and that brought to the surface the most powerful urges to flee of all.

"What's wrong?" Silas asked. "You've gone pale. I can see it even in this light."

I knew that this was one of those situations where I should demur, say something polite and reassuring, but there was no girlhood grooming to take over when my mind and tongue failed, and so the truth came out instead. "There are times when I doubt . . . when I doubt us. Our future. One moment, I think I can stay next to him forever, and then the next, I feel trapped by it. I feel terrified of *him* sometimes, that he'll wound my heart or betray me or—"

Or kill me. But grooming or no, I absolutely knew I shouldn't voice that last thought out loud, not to his closest friend.

But I couldn't not stay my tongue either—not completely. I had no one to talk to about this, no one to seek advice from. "The night he proposed," I said, keeping my eyes on the shadowed bedroom, worried that Mr. Markham would overhear, "he made me promise never to ask about the night Violet died. Why would he do that, Silas, if there wasn't something awful that he'd done? That he had to keep hidden from me?"

"Ivy," he started, but I cut him off, pacing.

"I should have said no. I can't agree to that; I can't not *know.* Because what if the rumors are true? What if he did kill her? And what if he kills me?"

Silas stared at me for a long moment, his face creased with deep unhappiness. His characteristic smile was absent when he asked, "Did I ever tell you I was at Markham Hall the night Violet died?"

It took a moment for his words to sink in. When they did, I turned and stared at him. "I didn't know. Nobody ever mentioned . . . "

"There were a lot of well-known people there that night, but Julian and the local police very thoughtfully excluded our presence from public knowledge to spare our reputations."

"I can't believe Mrs. Harold didn't tell the entire village," I said, more to myself than to Silas, thinking of Mrs. Harold's calculating gossip.

"Mrs. Harold?"

"The rector's wife?" I prompted. "Young with blonde hair? Slender? Talks incessantly?"

His eyes widened with recollection and something else— something that flashed all too briefly in those blue depths and then vanished. "I remember now," he said. "You know, she's grown up in the county too. She always had a thing for Julian, even after he married. Even after she herself got married. She was always finding excuses to hang around Markham Hall, I suppose hoping that Julian would finally notice her and give her all those things in bed that her feeble clergyman cannot."

"Anyway, what I wanted to tell you," he said, steering the conversation back to his revelation, "was that night, I saw how deeply unhappy Violet and Julian made each other. He had almost completely reformed himself for her—celibate while he courted her those three months, swearing off any other lovers.

But she didn't care. She wanted only to be back in London again, to be the belle of the *ton* again."

"And she was pregnant," I blurted. I hadn't meant to tell him, hadn't meant to bring it up at all, but it was such a shadow at the back of my mind, a shadow that changed everything.

Silas didn't look surprised. "I know," he said darkly. "I learned it that night."

"You did?" I knew it couldn't have been common knowledge, or Mrs. Harold would have told me all about it.

He nodded. "They fought at the dinner loudly, angrily. He wanted a divorce, she threatened to kill herself if he tried to sue for one. It was quite uncomfortable to listen to, so I suggested the other guests and I move into the parlor, farther away from them, and we all did, to give them more privacy. I was the last to leave the room, and so I believe I was the only one who heard her tell him."

"About the baby."

"Yes," he said, looking troubled. "About the baby."

"How could she threaten to kill herself when she knew she was pregnant?" I asked. "Even Violet is not that selfish."

"You know what I think? I think she was desperate. Think about it—both she and Julian knew the child couldn't be his. If he divorced her and let that be known, the shame would have destroyed her. Her life would have been over, and while I know Julian would have provided for her, she would have never been able to show her face in society again. *But* if she would have remained married, she would've still had the status of Markham Hall in addition to providing—what the world would have believed to be—a firstborn heir. Then she could have escaped and gone back to London through more polite, traditional means."

"So she had to stay married to him. No matter what." I chewed on the pad of my thumb as I pictured it all—Violet's fair face alight with fear and rage, Mr. Markham's rigid with anger and rejection.

"But she hated him," Silas reminded me. "Had it simply been a question of accepting his wife's sin—a sin that happened before their nuptials—then I have no doubt he would have accommodated. Raised the child as his own. But she made him acutely miserable, made it clear that she hated him and hated being married to him. She called him names I've never heard—even at school—not to mention she'd been sleeping with his valet, Gerald."

"Gareth," I corrected. "Why on earth does Mr. Markham keep him employed then? Surely that would be grounds for letting him go?"

Silas gave me another smile, rueful this time. "I suppose there was a sense of brotherly camaraderie in their suffering. You never saw Violet in her prime, did you? She was relentless and devastating, not to mention the mistress of the estate. No gentleman could have refused her. Certainly no servant in her employ. I think it was apparent from fairly early on that he had been coerced by the nature of his position to capitulating, and Mr. Markham felt sympathetic to that."

It was all so complicated, this mix of loyalties and betrayals. I couldn't keep track of who deserved my sympathy and who deserved my disregard, and I certainly couldn't keep straight how much fear I should allot to Mr. Markham himself.

And as much as I wanted to trust Silas, as much as I instinctively liked him, he was Mr. Markham's oldest friend. They shared a bed and they shared women—would they also not share and keep each other's secrets? How could I be certain that Silas wasn't deluded—or worse, lying to protect my future husband?

The sun was truly dawning now, pink and orange streaks radiating past the pitched roofs and gables of the city. More people crowded the streets, the din of wheels and voices beginning to soar above the paving stones to mingle with the birds chirping and the wind blowing past swinging signs and clustered chimneys.

"I am telling you this," Silas said, as if sensing my thoughts, "because most people don't know, but I think you deserve to. And Julian deserves your trust. See, after that horrific fight, she vanished. Disappeared. Julian joined us in the parlor, saying that Violet had gone to her room to rest, but would be down shortly. She never came."

"Did you look for her?"

"Yes. He didn't want to highlight her absence, so he waited until the guests had left, and he and I searched the house and grounds. The housekeeper helped too. That's when he told me that Violet had taunted him about her and Gareth, threatened to sleep with Gareth that very night to prove Mr. Markham's impotence when it came to following through on his threats of divorce. He was furious, expecting to come upon the two in every corner, and also terrified, because Violet had really sounded hysterical enough to hurt herself, and he worried for her safety."

"How could she say such things?" I wondered. "About Gareth, I mean, when her position was so tenuous? Surely she would be more calculating than that."

"She was like a cornered animal, ready to lash out at anything and anyone. For what it's worth, it deeply wounded Julian. Fidelity is something he prizes himself on—don't look so surprised, Miss Leavold—and he was unfailingly faithful to both Arabella and Violet."

"It's not hard to be faithful for a month," I said, more to myself than to Silas.

He heard anyway. "Don't be so suspicious. He would have been loyal to both of them until the end of his days. But it cuts both ways: he expected the same loyalty of Violet and she so blatantly refused. Yes, this understandably hurt and angered him very much."

Silas might have been trying to reassure me, but I felt anything but reassured in that moment. All he had conjured in my mind was the image of jealous wrath, of a bitter hurt that might not have thought twice about cutting a strap on a saddle.

"What I'm trying to say is that despite his anger and jealousy, Julian still searched everywhere. He still worried about her. And when we couldn't find her, he sent a servant to Scarborough to notify the constables and mobilize a larger search. We agreed to sleep for a few hours, and then resume looking at dawn."

"But she was dead by dawn."

"Yes."

Mr. Markham was stirring now, and the sound of his long limbs moving in the sheets made me drop my voice and step closer to Silas. "So you were apart from him for part of the night?"

"Yes, but Ivy, he couldn't have murdered Violet. What man searches for a woman in the frozen dark for hours, *sends for the police*, and then decides to kill her a couple hours later? What kind of man would do that?"

I didn't know. Because part of me didn't know what kind of man Mr. Markham was at all.

CHAPTER 6

*T*he rest of our sojourn in York was largely uneventful. Mr. Markham took me to the silk warehouse and then to a fashion house, where all manner of dress styles were presented to me. Shoes, a veil, jewelry, new underthings—the process of attiring a wealthy man's bride was as arduous as it was overwhelming, and I found myself deferring to Mr. Markham's choices because I simply did not care.

The only thing out of the ordinary that occurred was running—almost literally—into a strange man in our hotel lobby, where we had stopped to offload several hatboxes and other sundry items. Mr. Markham had been directing the porter to our room and I had been searching for the gloves I wanted to wear to dinner that night, when I felt legs brush against my skirt. I turned to see a short man, quite old, with clouds of white hair around his head.

"I beg your pardon," he said softly.

"No apology is necessary," I said and then went back to my search, assuming the encounter was over.

"Are you Ivy Leavold?"

I straightened, quite surprised. No one here in Yorkshire could possibly know me by sight, outside of the residents of

Stokeleigh and Mr. Markham's circle of friends. "Yes," I answered hesitantly. "I am she."

He nodded, a serene motion that indicated he had already known the answer, but was genuinely pleased to have heard it just the same. Everything about him seemed gentle, inoffensive. "Miss Leavold—"

"And you are?" Mr. Markham's voice came from beside me. I turned to see my betrothed giving the older gentlemen a look that was hard and cold, and clearly protective of me.

"My apologies," the man said, clearing his throat. And then as abruptly as we'd made contact, he bowed and left without a gesture or word of farewell. I stared after his surprisingly agile figure as he descended the hotel steps.

"Who was that man?" Mr. Markham asked.

I shook my head. "I've never seen him before in my life." The man in question was now completely gone from sight, having merged with the bustling sidewalk traffic. "But it was the strangest thing; he knew who I was. He knew my name was Ivy Leavold. Isn't that odd?"

Mr. Markham didn't answer. But a frown creased his face, and he wrapped a tight arm around me. He didn't let me out of his sight for the rest of the day, and several times I caught him glancing over his shoulder, as if he were worried that we were being followed.

* * *

"Let's elope to Gretna Green," I begged as we came out of yet another store. "Let's marry abroad. This is too much."

He turned to me then and caught my chin in his gloved fingers. "Ivy," he said, looking both amused and pained. "Must we have this fight every time I give you something? I'm not above taking you to the bank and showing you what is in the accounts there in order to stop this fretting about money."

"It's unnecessary," I said, but he moved his fingers to my lips.

"It's necessary to me," he said, voice gravelly. "Think of how generous you are being right now, indulging my selfish whim to dress you like a queen."

"But I'm *not* a queen," I protested.

"You are, wildcat," he said, and then I was pressed against the wall of the store we'd just left, his hips and chest pressing into me. "You are the queen of my mind." He moved his hips, and even through my dress, I felt his arousal. "Among other things . . ."

And then his mouth moved over me, kissing my lips and my nose and my jaw and the shell of my ear, and my protests melted away.

But I didn't forget that I wasn't the first bride to be purchasing silks and lace for a wedding to Mr. Markham. Two women had done the same before me, one of them perhaps in this very city, at these very shops, and I sensed her, a ghost trailing her fingers over unraveled bolts of fabric and over the sweet-smelling leather in the shoe shop.

If she could speak, would she warn me away? I felt her weighing on my mind as we jostled home in the carriage, as we slid our bodies together in Mr. Markham's bed.

He had loved her, Silas had said.

And I had to know that at least with her, at least with this poor, gentle, doomed girl, that his love had not ended in violence.

* * *

"I KNEW I'd find you down here."

I opened my eyes to see Mr. Markham pushing his way through the tall grass of the clearing, bluebells nodding sedately in his wake. His jacket was off and slung over his arm, and his sleeves were rolled up, exposing his lean, defined forearms.

We'd been back at Markham Hall for a couple of days, and this morning I'd decided to flee the dark corridors and brooding tapestries, seeking the bright yellow sun and high blue sky, soaking in the July sights and smells before it inevitably rained. I'd even brought a book with me—*Lorna Doone*—but couldn't focus on John and Lorna and Carver's feuding love triangle. Instead, my thoughts raced from Arabella to Violet to bolts of silk and lace, until the gentle breeze had lulled me into an uneasy peace, and I'd fallen into a warm, grassy doze.

Mr. Markham sat down next to me, his head blocking the sun, and I peered up at him, at the way the bright light framed him and cast his sharp, strong features into shadow. There was nothing about him to suggest violence or pain right now; his face was open and warm, and his eyes glowed with affection. Silas's words had done very little to reassure me, but seeing Mr. Markham like this did. I almost felt as if I *could* know him, know all of him and therefore trust him completely. And if I could know him, then maybe the ever-present doubts would finally evanesce and allow me to bask fully in my good fortune.

"Did you love Arabella?" I asked. I knew it was abrupt, impolite even, but I didn't care. I had to stitch together these pieces of his past. I had to know that he wouldn't grow tired of me, wouldn't grow to despise me. Wouldn't hurt me. If he had loved Arabella, as Silas had said, then maybe everything else that Silas had told me was true, and whatever secret Mr. Markham was keeping was something less horrifying than murder.

There was a flash of shock in his face, a quick downturn to his mouth, and for a moment, I thought he would shutter himself away again. But he didn't. Instead, he rearranged his long frame so that he was lying in between my legs, his head resting on my lower stomach, and he said, after getting comfortable, "Yes. Yes, I loved her."

"Silas said you did."

"Silas. Of course." He adjusted his head, putting pressure on my pelvis, and I was acutely aware of the fabric that separated his mouth from my sex. He kept talking, stroking my leg through my dress. "We knew each other a long time before we married, and we wrote frequently. When the family solicitors told me that it was time to settle down and ensure that Markham Hall had an heir, it never occurred to me not to marry the girl my father had intended. She was kind and intelligent and pretty, in a frail sort of way. I had always enjoyed her company. And yes, in those short weeks, I grew to love her."

"I'd heard it implied that you took her to Italy to intentionally exacerbate her illness."

I didn't need to see him to know that his jaw was clenching, that those stubbled cheeks were tensing with anger. "If they could have seen her—so lovely even as she could barely lift her head to speak—they wouldn't say such things. She was a saint; I could no more have harmed her than I could've harmed a child. We went to Italy because we had initially decided to honeymoon in Switzerland, and then the doctors in Geneva thought the warm Mediterranean air would help—to comfort her at least, if not to cure her. And it did seem to help, a little. She was awake and alert, at least, in her final days."

There was an exhale and then an uneven inhale. "Part of me died the day she died."

The breeze had stilled and so when he said those words, they hung heavy and laden in the air. It took me a minute to identify the difference between when he talked about Arabella and when he talked about Violet, but then I saw it. It was *sadness*. There was no guilt or torture or haunted remorse when it came to his first wife, only the memory of young love and keen loss.

I twined my fingers in his hair. "I'm so sorry," I whispered. "You deserved a happy and full life together."

"And you deserved living parents and a competent brother to take care of you." He turned so that he was almost prone in between my legs, his face cradled in the crease where my thigh met my hip. He peered up at me, looking so young and so vulnerable like this, and I felt my heart twist. I loved his strength and his weakness, his command of me and his dependence on me.

I loved him. I loved him to the point of the damnation of my soul.

And I was afraid of him.

"Why are you asking me about Arabella?" he asked, and he resumed stroking my legs, this time under my dress.

How could I tell him about my vast array of insecurities and fears? How could I confess that I was afraid that he would grow bored of me? That he might betray me, abandon me, or kill me? No. It was too ridiculous to voice out loud, as was the feeling that if I could claim his past, I could somehow claim a safe future for us.

We met gazes and his face grew serious. "Answer me, Ivy."

"I just wanted to know more about Arabella," I evaded. "You've talked of Violet, but never of her . . . "

A calloused hand was sliding up my thigh now. "It was fifteen years ago. I loved her, but memories fade with time, and I've had years to grow accustomed to the idea of her death." My skirts were pulled up unceremoniously, exposing the thin drawers I wore. "And, Ivy, you are lying to me."

"I—I am not lying—"

A loud smack reverberated through the meadow and I processed the noise before I processed the heat flaming on my flank. I gasped and looked at him. His dark brows had drawn together and his eyes were stern.

"Lie again and I'm taking you over my knee. Do you understand?"

I nodded, feeling the burn of his smack turn into molten sensation. For some reason, the idea of being taken over his knee seemed almost appealing.

My drawers were pulled off, and then my legs spread so that I was bare and open to his grim and determined face. Without warning, he jabbed two fingers inside of me, rough and probing, pinning my hips to the ground with his other hand. I writhed against the sudden invasion; I wasn't ready for it and I wasn't ready to answer his questions, no matter what methods he used to leverage the answers out of me.

"Why. Did. You. Ask," he said, punctuating each word with a thrust of his fingers.

I cried out, trying to squirm, but I didn't know if I was squirming away from him or toward him, because the rough pain had turned *oh-so quickly* into pleasure and suddenly I didn't want him to stop, not ever.

"You're wet now," he observed. "Does it arouse you to make me angry? To lie? To have me punish you?"

I moaned, because he had found that perfect spot inside that turned me at once tense and melting.

"It does. Such a bad girl. So filthy to find pleasure in such things." And then he took his fingers—slick with my own want —and slid one into my ass. I whimpered as he added a second and then used his other hand to caress my clit with feather-light touches.

"Please," I said raggedly. "I need to be fucked."

"Filthy," he repeated. He didn't move, just kept stoking that dark fire with his fingers and watching me writhe with a rigid, almost disciplinary, expression on his chiseled face. "Tell me why you asked, Ivy, or I swear to God, I will never let you come again."

"I . . . I was scared," I managed.

"Scared of what?"

I didn't answer for a moment. Even in the haze of pleasure, I realized that I was close to revealing something irrevocable, and that doing so carried a whole host of consequences—wounding him emotionally was but one. It didn't seem wise to alert the predator that I'd caught his scent; if I confessed that I was worried for my safety, would that alone seal my fate?

He pinched my clitoris and twisted, a bright, sharp tweak that elicited a noise I'd never heard from myself. "*Scared of what?*" he demanded.

"Of you," I whispered finally, tears spilling out of the corners of my eyes. "I'm scared of you."

Time seemed to freeze then. His mouth parted with surprise and his eyes widened. That wound I'd been afraid of creating—it was there, an almost visible slash across his chest. I regretted it all then, not just confessing to my fears, but to having them in the first place and maybe even to coming to Markham Hall at all. Then his eyes narrowed and his mouth pressed into a thin line.

"On your knees," he ordered.

I clambered to obey, tears still falling, desperate to make that brief look of pain a distant memory, desperate to show him how much I *did* love him, despite everything else.

"So you believe all the gossip then?" he breathed, standing up and walking around me. "That I'm in the habit of killing my wives? And you thought you'd make sure that, at the very least, I didn't kill *one* of them?"

I knew there was no point in lying now. I nodded, miserable with crying and also with the pulsing, unsated want between my legs. He came around behind me and laid his hands on my shoulders.

"Are you afraid now?" he asked. "We are alone, after all; I could kill you right here in this pasture and nobody would know." The jagged sarcasm in his words couldn't hide the bleakness in his voice. My heart split at that bleakness, wanted to heal it, cover over the parts of him that I had blighted with my admission.

His hands slid up and wrapped around my neck. I shivered, and there again was the pull of fear and desire, the adrenaline sending fast and painful throbs to my swollen cunt.

"Are you afraid now, wildcat?" he asked, his fingers tightening. "Afraid of me?"

"Julian," I murmured. "Please."

"Please what?"

His fingers were still loose enough that I could turn my head, and I did so now, looking back at him and wincing at his tortured expression. I only knew one thing that would help, the one thing that always helped us, the language our souls both spoke and demanded. "Fuck me," I pleaded. "Fuck me until this isn't here anymore."

This. This fight, this betrayal, this doubt. This ugly thing I'd nursed for more than two months and had now let free in a sunny meadow on a perfect afternoon. But he could get rid of it, my Julian could. He always did that, with his mouth and his fingers and his cock. He could drive us away from pain and into bliss, erase my doubts, if only temporarily. If only he would give it to us.

If only.

"Not this time, wildcat," he said. And he let go of me, stepping back.

No. No, that couldn't be it. We'd always shared our bodies with each other, sharing pleasure, giving and taking, our skin whispering what our words could not. And he was saying no? Even as the hard length of his cock was so erect, I could almost trace the veins through his trousers?

"No," he said again, reading the horror on my face. And then he said nothing else, scooping up his jacket and leaving me kneeling, weeping, among the bluebells and the rustling grass.

CHAPTER 7

I don't know how long I knelt there, slumped and sobbing, my heart rending itself into pieces. But the blue sky had silvered itself gray and the breeze had turned chilly and sharp by the time my tears finally subsided. I tried to stand, but my muscles screamed in protest—cramped from kneeling for so long—and I half fell over instead, curling onto my side and staring at the sky listlessly until I felt the muscles loosen and relax.

But even then, it was hard to find the motivation to stand. I would stand up and walk back to . . . to what? To Mr. Markham, angry and cold? Or to an empty house, bereft of his presence? Certainly, it would be to an empty bed, and I couldn't stand that. Not when I needed him more than ever.

I stood shakily, wondering when the independent and free-willed Ivy Leavold had become this wreck of a girl who could barely walk. When had I traded my reason for madness? Because it could only be madness, this feeling that drove me toward Julian Markham. Despite what Silas had said, the police and the county were convinced that Mr. Markham had killed my cousin. What's more, he had expressly forbidden me from asking about her death. All the evidence—the testimony of others and his own behavior—pointed to his guilt.

So why did I continue to pine for him? My body craved him, yes, but it was my mind and my soul that ached and thrashed the most without him. I hated myself for hurting him, for making him leave, yet I hated him too for leaving, for giving me no other choice, no other way. *If only he'd confided in me from the beginning,* I wished vehemently, then stopped. It didn't do any good now. He'd done everything he could to keep Violet's death shrouded in mystery and that was why we were here now.

Alone.

Apart.

Furious with each other.

As I walked, my anger gained greater and greater strength. *How dare he act as if he is the victim? As if I am the one acting egregiously?* He was the one suspected of murder, the one keeping secrets. How could he expect me to stand by and absorb his darkness without reacting to it?

He wanted me to be like Arabella. But I couldn't. I could only be Ivy.

I wandered through the woods until the rain started, a drizzle that brought with it an early dusk, and by the time I made it to the house, my dress was wet and muddy and my hair was plastered to my head in tangled strands. It didn't signify; there was no one waiting up indoors, not even a servant. They'd all retired early, I supposed, not one of them thinking to save a dinner for me . . . or even to come looking for me.

I barely existed here. I was a ghost before I was even dead.

I peeled off my dress in my room, not bothering to change into anything else, and went to Mr. Markham's chambers. I knew he wasn't there—from the moment I'd stepped into the house, I'd recognized that empty stillness that was characteristic of his absence—but my chest still ached when I saw the empty room, bedspread pulled taut as if the rumples and wrinkles from our morning lovemaking had never happened.

There was no fire, and a chill was seeping in through the windows and walls, so I slid under the covers of his bed, tears burning anew at the scent of the soap he had sent up from London. That smell, more than anything else, reawakened the heavy pulsing in my sex, a pulsing made all the worse for the tangled emotions surrounding it.

I knew it was no substitute, but it was mindless need more than anything that drove my hand in between my legs. I ran my fingertips over the soft folds, imagining it was Julian doing it with hungry eyes and an even hungrier mouth. I breathed in the fresh male scent that clung to the sheets and began circling my clit, hard and fast, thinking of him thrusting into me in this very bed. Thinking of the way his cufflinks had gleamed in the restaurant as he fucked my cunt with his fingers. Of the way he'd owned me today in the field, of the arresting way he took control of my body and used it against me.

I buried my face in the pillow as I came, crying out from the all-too-brief flash of pleasure and also from the concurrent ache of emptiness that came with it. It didn't matter how roughly I touched myself or how many orgasms I created—it wasn't the same. It wasn't him.

And what if it never was again?

* * *

I SLEPT LATE. Deep and late, with no dreams, but the keen aware-ness of loss welcomed me the moment that the opiate of sleep wore off. I was alone in my future husband's bed, with no way of knowing if he would still consent to be my husband. I had been afraid that he was going to kill me, but the morning brought with it an even clearer realization—I was afraid of losing him more than I was afraid of him hurting me. *Perfect love casts out all fear*, I recalled my childhood curate saying—and my love was far from perfect. But it was still trying valiantly, a bird beating the air with broken wings.

I wasn't hungry and I didn't want to dress. Instead, I left the bed to curl up on an armchair near the window so I could watch the wet world outside and think.

I wanted Julian. I wanted to fuck him and fight him, and I wanted to nestle by his side at night. I wanted more nights like two nights ago—where he'd woken me by whispering poetry in my ear, chanting Keats and Shelley and Blake as he wrenched climax after climax from my body. I wanted more days like our last day in York, where we had held hands in the street and argued over which restaurant to eat at for dinner.

But I couldn't have Julian the way I wanted with Violet's grave between us. One way or another, I would have to find out the truth. No more shoving suspicions to the back of my mind, no more avoiding the topic as if her name alone would burn our lips. I would have to either torture him or coax him into telling me about that night. . . and then I would face any problems I found once I got to them. For now, I needed to focus on how to extract the truth to begin with.

But how? Mr. Markham was impenetrable, a fastness of determination and silence. There was no way I could tug the truth loose from him, not if all the policemen and dark whispers in the county couldn't.

I worried at my lower lip while I thought, trying to ignore the voice that whispered *or you could run.* But the voice grew louder and louder, until I jumped to my feet and started pacing, my feet digging into the plush rug as I walked.

Run.

Run.

Run.

You don't need to pry the truth from him, the voice said. *You only need to protect yourself.* I could leave, now, perhaps apply to Solicitor Wickes in London to help me find a position someplace...

But I didn't *want* to. I wanted to stay here, in this haunted medieval manor, with its equally haunted owner. I wanted to be his wife. I wanted to be *his.*

Run, the voice said, brooking no argument, and exhausted from the war between my two selves—the one that belonged to Mr. Markham and the one that listened to reason—I ran.

* * *

IT TOOK ONLY a moment to dress, to pull on my old boots and find my purse. I had no plan—not even a direction—but somehow I knew I needed to leave. Not forever and maybe not even for the entire day, but for a few hours at least. I couldn't think clearly while I was here, couldn't order my thoughts before a thousand memories had them spinning off into frantic circles again. Had it been less than three months that I'd been resident here? And yet how pregnant with recollection was every corner, every tread in the staircase, every chair that had once held the sprawling, powerful form of Mr. Markham.

I told myself I wasn't leaving for good, but I dressed in one of my old dresses and left any and all trinkets in my room— including Julian's ring, my engagement ring—which felt heavy and wrong on my slender fingers, knowing I wouldn't be able to decide anything while I was so materially connected to him. I put no thought to money, no thought to travel, only to fleeing, for however long it took for me to think.

Guilt flashed through me as I shut the bedroom door, hiding the gleaming ring from sight. What if Mr. Markham came back and found me gone? What if I hurt him even more?

No, I thought in response to the thought. *He doesn't have that right.* Why should I be the one to stay, when he'd already left? Why should I be the one to bridge the gap, to hold fast to our promises, when he hadn't shown any inclination to do so himself?

And why should any reasonable person want to woo a suspected murderer back into her bed?

I passed no one on my way to the front door, and the front courtyard was empty of horses and people. It was nothing but wet flagstones and weather that was somewhere between drizzle and mist. I plunged into the fog, grateful to be swallowed up and grateful to see that Markham Hall had been swallowed up behind me. But the tightness in my chest didn't ease and my mind didn't clear. I could only think ahead to my next footfall, to my next breath.

Run, that voice urged. *Run until you can't any longer.*

I walked still, finding it impossible to gauge distance or time in the fog, worried I'd missed the fork in the road that went to the village and had instead taken the road that would eventually bring me up to the moors.

Hooves pounded the road behind me, and I whirled around, seeing nothing but fog and grasping tree branches. Then the gray mist parted to reveal Mr. Markham and Raven, the former with a loosely knotted cravat and tousled hair.

Run! the voice screamed. *Run while you can!*

And I did step back warily as Mr. Markham dismounted his horse and walked toward me, slowly, his hands out as if he were approaching a wild animal. "Where are you going?" he asked, and there was palpable pain in his words. "Are you leaving here? Leaving me?"

His eyes dropped down to my hand—my now naked hand—and something inside of him seemed to shred itself apart, flay itself open. He met my eyes again and that look was enough to make me weep. "You *are* leaving," he whispered.

I half shook my head, but I took another step back as I did. "You left first," I answered, also in a whisper. Our voices hung in the air like the mist: too light to fall, too heavy to float.

"I had business in town," he said. "I heard someone was seeking a meeting with me, and I needed to send a message to York to arrange it."

"And that took until today?"

A muscle leapt in his jaw. "I'll confess to needing some time alone before I felt myself contained."

"Am I not allowed the same?"

Resolve steeled in his eyes and in a handful of steps, he crossed to me, too fast for me to evade. One arm was around me and then the other between us, his hand gripping my jaw and forcing me to look up at him.

"I left to cool off, Ivy Leavold. But why are you leaving now? Can you honestly tell me that you were planning on coming back?"

I couldn't. I hadn't left knowing it was for good, but I *had* left knowing it was a possibility that I might not return.

I saw the moment this registered with him. His eyes went even harder. "I just came from the house. I searched every room for you. And you know what I found?"

I didn't answer, couldn't answer.

"You slept in my bed last night," he breathed. "Tell me, Ivy, were you naked when you slept in my bed? Did you touch yourself? Did you make yourself come?"

Almost against my will, I nodded. I couldn't resist the pull of those viciously hungry eyes.

He groaned at my response. "Tell me," he said, shoving his hips against mine. "Tell me what you did."

"I could smell you," I said. "I could smell you on the bed. I couldn't stop myself, I had to come. I rubbed myself thinking of you."

"Thinking of my cock? Or my tongue? Or my fingers?"

"Yes. All of it. All of you."

He buried his face in my neck and breathed me in, his arm tightening around me. "Why are you trying to leave?" he asked, the words muffled. "What can I do to make you stay?"

His arms were so strong around me, his voice so rough and husky, and I knew if I looked at his face, I would see those lightly scruffed cheeks and those piercing green eyes. My body and soul longed to submit to him, to be subsumed by this man, this force of nature that could light my skin on fire with a single touch. But my mind—my mind remained crouched and wary, prey darting around a trap. And that's why I could tell him, "I'll only stay if I know I will be safe."

"Safe," he repeated. "*Safe.*" I expected his hold on me to loosen, for him either to be offended or suspicious, but instead, he held me closer, one hand deftly pulling up my skirts. "What does that really mean, wildcat? Safe from me? Or safe from your own fears?"

I'd dressed so hastily that I hadn't bothered with drawers and so his fingers found my cunt easily.

"You're wet," he remarked, lifting his head from my neck to speak into my ear. "Tell me, are you wet because you feel *safe* with me right now? When you make yourself come in my bed, are you thinking about how *safe* I make you feel?"

God, I *was* wet. And I was growing wetter, my nipples hardening into painful points beneath my dress. His fingers flicked gently across my swelling bud, tracing delicate curves along my sex.

"So what is it, Ivy? What kind of safety do you so desire that you are running away from me?"

I was breathing harder and faster now, arching my hips into his hand. "I don't want you to hurt me."

He bit my neck—*hard*—and I cried out, bucking my pelvis even more as the pain sizzled into a fresh wave of arousal. "I think you like being hurt."

My mind was slipping away from me, burdened by my undeniable need and my insatiable longing for the man with his hand up my skirt.

But I managed to say it. Bluntly. "I'm afraid you'll kill me."

That did make him loosen his grip. "Kill you?" he demanded, seizing me tightly again, his thumb now pressing hard against my clitoris. "You are the most beautiful and the most perfect thing that's ever happened to me. I would slice my own throat before I hurt you."

My cunt—still achingly deprived from yesterday—swelled and pulled under the expert ministrations of his fingers. I spread my legs, trying to ride his hand, not caring that we were in the middle of the road to Stokeleigh and that anyone could happen by. "But Violet," I managed. "You hurt Violet."

All at once, the hand was gone. I made a noise of protest, but he stepped away, now standing out of reach. I could see his formidable cock tenting his pants, but he ignored whatever discomfort it gave him, his gaze steady against mine.

"Ivy, I am only going to say this once, because the night Violet died, I did something terrible—something so outside of my own character and the character of a gentleman that it gives me pain to recall. And it would give you pain to know, personally and also on behalf of your relation. But I need to say this, and you need to hear it: *I did not cut that saddle.* I had nothing to do with it, directly or indirectly."

His defense was so specific, so targeted to that one thing— the saddle—that it did almost nothing to allay my fears. I took a moment to phrase my next question, trying to ignore the pounding pulse of my clitoris as my pussy begged for release. "Did you have anything to do with her death, Julian? Anything at all?"

Julian. As soon as I uttered his name, I saw the chink in his armor, as if it were a weapon he could not resist. He hung his head. "Yes," he said after a long moment. "I won't lie to you. I had something to do with it. But I didn't cut her saddle."

I exhaled. Part of me wanted to use his honesty as evidence of his innocence—if he was willing to admit that he had played a part in her death, then surely he'd have admitted to cutting the saddle if he'd done it. But the other part of me recognized evasion and equivocation when I saw it; Mr. Markham may not be lying, but he was omitting key details of that night and at the same time, forestalling any future conversation about it.

"I don't know if that's good enough," I told him. "I need to know everything. I need to know exactly how you are guilty."

He stepped forward again, looking frustrated. He turned away and took a few paces, running his hands through his thick hair. He turned back to me. "How about this: You stay with me here at Markham Hall. You share my bed and my soul and my money and anything else I happen to own. And if I push you too far, if I frighten you beyond what you can bear, then you are free to leave, with as much money and security as you would need to live sumptuously the rest of your days."

"I don't want to live sumptuously. I want to know the truth."

He shook his head. "You think you do. But once you learn it, there's no unlearning it. There's no going back. I can live with you fearing me. But I can't live with you despising me."

"If I stay . . . " The idea was growing easier and easier to consider. "Will I ever get to know the truth?"

He took a deep breath, glancing down at the fog swirling around his feet. "Yes," he said. There was palpable reluctance in his tone, reluctance and resignation. "After we return from our honeymoon. I want to show you exactly how I will treat you as my own wife, my own soul, before you discover the blackest mark on my record."

"And I will still be able to leave, if what I learn is too much?"

His jaw tensed, but he nodded. "Yes. You will be free to leave at any point. Whether it is after our honeymoon or thirty years from now." His eyes softened. "I cannot cage you. I see that now. You may let me leash you and spoil you, use you and please you, but the moment you feel the cage coming down, you will startle and flee. That is your limit, Ivy. And I wish I would have known it sooner."

I was falling forward into his words, dizzy with the rush of relief and longing that swept through me. He would let me leave at any time. He *would* tell me the truth, and relatively soon. And finally, I could relent to the keening cry of my heart to be next to him. Because I loved him. Because I was made to be with him. And if I ever had to leave him, it would rend me into pieces.

CHAPTER 8

"*D*o we have an agreement?"

I didn't hesitate. I was done running from him. For now, at least.

"Yes," I said. "We have an agreement."

"Perhaps it would be helpful if we arranged a signal between us, something that would alert me to your need to stop or to leave." He came closer, and he pulled my hands into his. "That way, if the time ever comes, you won't have to think of what to say and you won't have to say anything more."

"Like what kind of signal?"

He let go of my hands and pressed his fingers against my lips. Instinctively I opened my mouth to nip and lick at them, tasting myself as I did so. My body began thrumming desperately for him once more.

"What's your favorite flower?"

"Bluebells," I replied, thinking of the way they had bobbed and rustled around Mr. Markham in the meadow yesterday.

He slid a finger into my mouth and I sucked on it eagerly, wishing it were his cock. "*Bluebell*, then. Remember that, Ivy. When you say that to me, I shall stand aside and let you leave, even as it kills me inside."

He pressed up against me, grinding his erection into my corseted stomach. "And if I ever push you too far in your education, if I ever make you feel only pain and no pleasure, use that word then as well. When I hear *bluebell*, I will stop immediately. That is the signal you will use to tell me if I have gone too far and you need to stop. That and no other word, do you understand?"

I nodded.

"Say yes, Ivy."

"Yes."

He rucked up my skirt, exposing my stockinged legs and bare pussy. His whole face darkened with lust. "Now," he growled. "We need to address the fact that you are not wearing your ring. Not to mention that I found you on the road, walking away from me."

I felt tears burn at my eyes—tears not of sadness or fear, but of unequivocal relief. This—this was how we were meant to be together. Him demanding, me yielding; me fighting and him relishing the fight.

"I won't apologize for leaving," I said, lifting my chin. "Especially since you left first."

"Don't test me." His eyes were on my legs and sex, still open to the air. "Or I will show you exactly what it's like to be afraid of me."

He palmed my cunt—hard—and my knees weakened. "How am I to teach you if you are going to play truant?" he continued. "Should a teacher not discipline a wayward pupil?"

"Not if the pupil didn't do anything wrong," I shot back. But my fierce words were belied by my body, which was melting under his possessive touch.

"What is your signal, wildcat?" he asked calmly.

"Bluebell," I answered, confused. *Didn't we just talk about this—*

I was pushed suddenly to the ground. The air was knocked from my lungs and I didn't have time to catch it again before he was on top of me, his mouth sealed over mine. He had never treated me so roughly, never pushed me, and everything in me struggled not to escape, but to push him back. To fight back.

Bluebell, my mind remembered.

But no. I didn't want to stop. I wanted to conquer him.

I scratched at his neck and he groaned, reaching up to pin my wrist above my head. He did the same with my other arm until both wrists were held fast to the ground by one of his hands. I thrashed underneath him, half wanting to buck him off, half desperate for any friction against my aching center, and the more I thrashed, the wilder he looked, until he was yanking his trousers open and pulling out his swollen member. I rolled to the side, thinking I'd manage to get on top of him, but my shoulder was slammed back into the ground, and before I could move or even think, his knees were in between my legs and he thrust inside of me so roughly that I saw static at the edges of my vision, as he seated himself fully in one stroke.

I was wet, but not entirely ready, and I felt the searing heat of him as he dragged himself back out and slammed into me again. "You lay still and take your punishment," he growled at me, driving into me with another powerful thrust. The weight of his body against my clitoris and the flexing of his hips in between my thighs sent spikes of desire to my core, but the whole scene —us rutting in the road like animals, him restraining my arms and forcing himself on me—it aroused me even further. Of course, he wasn't truly forcing himself—he had made sure that I remembered how to make him stop. But the illusion of struggle scratched an itch deep inside of me. The truth was that I was furious with him and furious with myself for loving him and furious with Violet for finding him first and then dying and making everything so complicated. I wanted to bite him and scratch him and pull his hair; I wanted to expend all this pent-up anger and pain on his body and score his psyche like he had scored mine.

And maybe part of me enjoyed being punished. No one since my parents had bothered to take care of me, emotionally, financially or otherwise, and I had prided myself on being independent, but there was something so primally comforting about ceding control. When he mastered me, I felt a burden lift that I didn't even know was there, the burden of emotional self-sufficiency and isolation. And that's why he was right—I did like him dangerous and unsafe. Because, however perverse it might be, when he took my body, he was showing me that he was going to take care of me, in all the ways that I needed.

And what was that feeling, if not safety?

This realization stunned me. I went slack underneath him as I tried to process it, taking in how perfectly the jagged edges of our souls interlocked, how perfectly he had known me even when I hadn't known myself. He had always seen this in me, this need to be mastered, and he had given it, as he had given me his heart.

And I could see it now, his heart, as he thrust into me with everything he had, as his eyes glossed with what could only be unshed tears. I watched them as they fell and I licked them off my lips as they dripped onto my mouth.

"You're crying," I whispered.

He stopped moving, his head hanging in between his muscular shoulders. "Yes," he said thickly. "I almost lost you." He met my eyes, his green ones lanced with pain. "I need you, Ivy. And the idea of life without you . . . I can't stand it."

He let go of my wrists and then slid his hands under my waist and lifted me up. We were still joined together, and I now rested on his lap, my skirts bunched up around us. He laid his head against my breast as I started moving and wriggling on top of him, trying to grind my clitoris against his pubic bone. "Why do I need you so much?" he asked, his voice quieted by my chest. "Why do I want to cherish you and break you at the same time?"

"I don't know," I said, my voice wavering as I worked myself on his shaft, feeling heat creep up my neck. "But I feel the same way about you. I want you to cherish me and to break me too. I want to rage at you and serve you. Oh, Julian," I moaned as my channel stroked his cock. "Try to break me now. Please."

His grip on my waist tightened and I felt his cock swell impossibly hard inside of me. He was hesitating, I saw, resisting that dark urge inside of him, and I didn't know how to show him it was okay, that I needed that part of him right now or I would fly apart in doubt.

"I remember our signal," I told him, as gently as I could while I rocked back and forth in his lap. "But please, hurry, I—"

And then I was on my back again and he was kneeling, holding my hips up and driving into my pussy as if I weighed nothing, as if he were using my pussy the same way he used his silk handkerchief—to get himself off with no other consideration.

"I am going to fuck you here in the road," he said, each thrust slamming the head of his cock deep, deep inside. "I'm going to mark you with my cum. And then I'm dragging you back to the house, and I am going to fuck you until you know what it really means to be punished. Perhaps I'll fuck more than your pussy, tonight. Hmm?"

I moaned with want at the thought, my clitoris throbbing with the idea of being treated so roughly, of his thick cock taking me wherever he wished it to.

"Does that make you wet? Me fucking your ass? Only sluts like to be fucked that way. Are you a slut, Ivy?"

I moaned again, incoherent with need, my orgasm building inexorably in my pelvis as Mr. Markham pounded into me again and again. "Little sluts have to be punished," he grunted. "And fucked until their greedy little cunts are satisfied." His fingertips dug into the soft flesh of my ass, hard enough to bruise, and I loved it, panting as the bright points of pain counterweighted the pleasure.

"I know you want to come on my dick. Show me how a little slut can't help but come whenever she's being fucked like she deserves."

And then he ground my pussy against him, hard and fast, my bud rubbing against him and the head of his cock rubbing against the secret spot deep inside.

His eyes met mine, and his face was uncontrolled—uncivilized even—pure triumph and lust painting his sharp features as he watched me come unraveled. My pussy contracted and then exploded with sensation, vivid release ripping through me, making my back arch so far off the ground that only my shoulders still made contact with the road. I writhed against it, trying to ride it out, but I had no control of my body—my hips were still firmly in Mr. Markham's hands and raised up to his cock as he knelt. He held still as I clenched around him, his eyes fluttering closed. "Ah, *fuck*. That's good, Ivy," he breathed. "You come so good. I can feel it squeezing me."

And then he drew my hips back and impaled himself in me again, his body staying stationary while he used my sated pussy like the rest of me was inconsequential.

Then he abruptly let go, pulling out and fisting his cock, slick and wide and almost purple in its near-climax.

"Show me your cunt," he ordered and I spread my legs wide. With a muttered *fuck*, he jerked himself once, twice, violently hard, and a stream of semen shot onto my pussy.

"Now your tits," he said and his voice was tight with the effort it took to control his orgasm. I hurriedly pulled down my bodice as far as it would go, exposing the tops of my breasts and the barest pink of nipple. Another rough stroke and he marked me there. "Your mouth," and this was now barely a strangled rasp. I opened wide, and with a long panting breath, he jerked himself to completion, lacing my lips and my neck and my tongue with his ownership.

His cock stayed hard and red, and the lust in his face was barely dimmed as he sat back on his heels and looked at me, with my skirts above my waist and all marked like his property.

"Where do you belong?" he asked.

"Here."

"Whom do you belong to?"

"You." And the answer was so easy, so natural, that I couldn't believe I had fought it these past few days. And as for his role in Violet's death—I would worry about that when the time came. For now, all I had to do was revel in his possession of me and my possession of him in return.

He rose from the road, and without bothering to tuck his still-erect dick back into his trousers, he picked me up and carried me over to Raven, who had been grazing patiently all this time. He climbed into the saddle, then easily lifted me in front of him. I stroked his exposed member as he turned Raven toward home.

"The servants will see," I said as we rode back into the courtyard.

"I don't care. I want them to know how hard you make me. And when they hear your screams tonight, they'll know how satisfied I make you."

True to his word, he dismounted and helped me down into his arms and carried me inside, his cock buried in my skirts and my skirts still tangled with my petticoats.

"About punishing me more tonight . . . Did you mean what you said, in the road?" I asked as we bypassed the stairwell and walked toward the library.

Julian looked at me and then leaned his head down to speak in my ear.

"I meant every fucking word."

CHAPTER 9

*N*o fire had been lit in the library, as it was midday, but the damp weather seemed to pervade the room, and I shivered as we stepped inside.

"Are you cold?" he asked.

"A little. I'll be fine."

He set me down on a damask sofa. "Fine's not good enough for my wildcat." He dropped a kiss on my forehead and went to draw up the fire. I watched him as he knelt and laid wood on the andiron, his long legs folded underneath him, his powerful arms straining the fabric of his shirt and jacket.

His motions were smooth and assured as he lit the fire, using newspaper to light the slender kindling sticks. When the logs finally caught, he set down the poker and turned toward me.

"Go get your engagement ring," he said, "and bring it down."

I bit my lip, feeling the first ripple of apprehension mingle with my anticipation. I felt boneless and relaxed and eager for more, but the engagement ring reminded me that Mr. Markham wasn't finished fulfilling my request to break me. I had fissured his usual control and composure, and I didn't know what the coming hours would bring, save for him penetrating me in that forbidden place. And even as the thought made my sex pulse

91

with want, it terrified me, this new boundary Mr. Markham was breaching.

I shivered again, not from cold this time, and left the library, straightening my dress as I went up the stairs in case I encountered anybody as I did. I didn't, although I heard the voices of some maids as they tended to a bedchamber down the hall. I took my ring and returned to the library, where Mr. Markham sat on the sofa awaiting me. He had one arm flung along the back of the sofa and the other lazily stroking his cock, his eyes glued to me as soon as I entered.

"Bring the ring here," he said, and I obeyed, dropping the ring into his outstretched palm. "Now go lock the door. We are not to be interrupted."

I realized my hands were shaking as I turned the ornate key in the lock. Was I excited or was I scared?

And given what I had realized about myself—and about *us*—did it matter which?

I turned and faced him, my fiancé and master, pressing my back against the door. Blood and warmth and want pooled in my core as I watched him watching me. His hand moved slowly over his shaft, which was thick and rigid, and his other hand held the ring, which sparkled in the silver light coming in through the tall windows. He was so magnificent, with his male organ so prominent and demanding, with his long legs and sun-browned hands and square jaw.

"Come over here."

I did, but I moved slowly, warily. The sex on the road had been stark and raw, an encounter that had soothed something inside of me, his fucking an alchemy that transmuted my days-long torment into a bliss I could've never imagined. But I was still nervous about being punished further. I didn't naturally crave pain or gravitate toward it, any more than I craved any other illness or injury. I knew Mr. Markham would take care of me, even as he claimed every inch of my body as his own. I knew that everything he did, he ultimately did for me.

But still, my steps were slow.

Bluebell, I reminded myself. *Bluebell bluebell bluebell.*

He watched me with amusement as I came before him and stood in between his parted legs. "Undress," he said as I shifted my weight.

He had seen me naked so many times before, but somehow this time was different. Perhaps it was knowing what was coming, knowing that I was still being punished. Perhaps it was the look in Mr. Markham's eyes—stern and arrogant all at once. Or maybe it was the ring that he spun casually in his fingers, the symbol of our promise—the symbol of my decision to stay, despite everything.

I unbuttoned my dress clumsily, shucking it and my petticoat —both liberally sprinkled with mud and leaves from our inter-lude in the road—and then pulled off my stays and chemise. Off came my boots, and when I reached for my garters, Mr. Markham reached up and stopped me. "Allow me," he said and leaned forward. I felt his warm breath on the inside of my thigh as he took the fabric gently between his teeth and tugged it down over my knee. He did the same on the other side, and I couldn't suppress a shudder as he pressed his lips to the sensitive skin on the side of my knee, his mouth hot and soft even through the silk. He leaned back and very deliberately set the ring on the end table, the diamond pointing toward the fire and sending prisms arcing across the thick leather spines of the books.

I stared at it now as he used both hands to ease my stockings down my calves, taking each foot onto his lap as he peeled the silk away, kissing my ankle, and then setting it gently back on the floor.

"You are so beautiful," he murmured, tracing a long finger from my foot all the way up to my sex. "And you were made for fucking."

I smiled slightly, recalling him speaking those same words on the night we'd first lain together. He slid his hands around the backs of my thighs and up to the curve of my ass, pulling me closer to his face. The sofa was low enough that his nose brushed against my pubic bone, and then he nuzzled his face into me, seeking my heat with his lips and tongue. The moment he tasted me, he made a noise of pleasure in the back of his throat, as if I were a feast he'd been starving for. As if my taste were the single most delicious and perfect thing he'd ever known.

He held me tight against his face, not letting me move, even as my nipples peaked and my clitoris swelled and my hips began jerking of their own accord. He loved on me, sucking on my bud until it felt ready to burst, like ripe fruit, licking at my folds until I felt wild with the need for more.

I arched my back and laced my fingers through his hair, tugging on it in sharp yanks I couldn't control. I rubbed myself against his face shamelessly, all thoughts falling away except for the need to climax, the need to drive his tongue deeper and faster into me. His stubble burned and scratched at the inside of my thighs, a luscious contrast to the soft silky hair twined around my fingers, and as I pictured the chafed red skin of my inner thighs, the way I would look marked and used after he was finished with me, I felt my climax rush in.

"I'm going to come," I panted, grinding my pussy against his face. "I'm going to—"

He wrapped his hands around my hips and pulled me firmly away from his face. My orgasm hovered like a mirage, shimmering waves that were just out of reach. I cried out, my body fighting to get closer to him, struggling against his iron grip. He looked up at me, his beryl eyes unforgiving.

Unyielding.

"No, Miss Leavold. No orgasm for you just yet, I'm afraid."

I must have looked incredulous or defiant or both, because his expression changed into something rougher, more implacable.

94

"You *are* going to be a good girl while you take your punishment, correct?"

I dug my fingernails into his hands, trying to pry them off my hips. "Not if you're going to be like this," I said, my voice protesting and plaintive. I knew I had no power here. I knew that I *wanted* to have no power here. But resisting felt so natural, as natural as submitting when Julian's will finally overcame my own. I dug deeper, no plan except to release his hold on me and maybe bring myself off with my own hand.

He didn't wince, even though I knew I had broken the skin in a few places. Rather, he let go of my hips and seized my hands in a fierce one-handed grip, tight enough that I had no hope of struggling free, but not quite tight enough to bruise. I tried pulling backwards, leaning my body weight into the effort, while he used his other hand to unknot his tie and slide the fabric from his neck. Once I realized what he had planned, I pulled harder and harder, squirming and twisting to get away, but it was no use. In a matter of seconds, my wrists were bound with silk, and he was standing before me, eyes burning with anger and his member still very erect, the wide tip flaring with unabashed need.

"You are quite the wayward pupil today," he said, unamused. He laced one hand in my hair, dislodging the pinned braids and twists that I had hastily thrown up this morning, and then dragged me over to the table like a cat by the scruff of the neck. He bent me over it, pressing my face against the cool, glossy wood.

"You consented to be my student, did you not?" he asked.

I couldn't nod, not with the way he had my head pinned, but I squeaked out a *yes.*

"You consented and then you removed your ring and tried to leave. I can't let that stand, Ivy. I cannot."

And then there was a sharp *crack* and a stinging burn that rocked my entire body. I cried out, moaning into the wood, searching for the right word to say, and then there was another *crack* and I shrieked, the flash of pain taking me more by surprise than the first.

He was spanking me. He was bending me over and slapping my bare ass with his hand. The word I needed—the word I was desperate to say—finally filtered through the pain. *Bluebell.* But at the same moment, I felt the wetness between my legs.

I was so aroused that I was almost dripping. I moaned again, not from pain this time, but from want. And did I want him to spank me again? I decided that I did.

I turned my head as much as I could, my mouth meeting his thumb, and I bit down as hard as I could. He hissed in anger, snatching his hand away, but he didn't spank me again.

"I know what you want, wildcat. You may resist my teachings, but you can't hide that greedy cunt from me. You want me to turn this beautiful ass red and glowing, and one day, I promise you, I will. You will learn to take your discipline any way I choose to dole it out." He ran a hand from my neck down to my lower back, his touch soft and loving. "You are so beautiful right now, Ivy, bent over for me. I love it when you think you can fight me. But I will love it even more when you have succumbed to your discipline and you take your lesson with eagerness."

He stepped behind me, so close that I could feel the fabric of his trousers on the back of my legs, and then without warning, he rammed into me, sheathing himself in one rough thrust. I was wet, but still not entirely ready, and so the thrill of pleasure I felt was serrated and jagged, the kind of feeling that curled my toes and hardened my nipples and clenched my core.

"Fuck, you're tight," he said, and in his words was a slender crack in his armored control. He bent over me as he sawed in and out, kissing my shoulders and biting my back in ferocious bites, as if he wanted to devour me whole. I shuddered and rocked into him, his touch driving me wild. He took my hips in his hands and then swiftly kicked my legs apart to widen his access—and to let him plunge deeper. The wider stance meant I could barely touch the floor, and so he held me up by the hips, driving into me relentlessly as my toes scrabbled for purchase on the carpet.

"Ivy, I feel your pussy swelling. It's getting tighter and tighter and there—your fingernails on the table. You're about to gouge the surface." He leaned in and rasped in my ear. "If you come without my permission, I will flay your ass raw and withhold your pleasure for days . . . or weeks. That trip to York will seem like child's play in comparison to the deprivation I can wreak."

His cock was so big—so big and so hard—and the way he had me lifted up meant that the wide head of his dick was stroking the irresistible spot inside. The spot that turned off my brain and made me into a rutting animal.

"I can't stop," I said breathily. "You . . . you're too good and your cock . . . oh Julian, it's making me feel so good."

"*Fuck.*"

His name. It was his name that did it. I often forgot it was my best weapon; for whatever reason, it undid him, snagging at the cracks in his control. With a growl that bordered on a roar, he pulled out and grabbed me by the back of my neck— truly like a cat this time, snatching me off the table and forcing me over to the tall windows against the far wall. My bound hands made it nearly impossible to avulse myself from his grip.

He took my silk-wrapped wrists and lifted them high above my head. "What are you—" And then I was pressed—no, *smashed* —against the cold, cold glass, pressed from my swollen clitoris to my breasts to my cheek, which was turned to the side. The window was a cold shock to my system, and my nipples beaded uncomfortably as goose bumps raced across my skin. My climax retreated, oh-so slowly, as painful as withdrawing a splinter from the skin. I whined against the glass, my breath creating fogged clouds that advanced and disappeared, advanced and disappeared, hypnotic in the way they matched the pounding of my heart.

"You will not come until I say." Another stinging slap across my backside. "Is that clear, Miss Leavold?"

I nodded slowly, feeling almost like a snake under the charm of a pipe-player. My conscious mind tried valiantly to make sense of all the pushes and pulls of Mr. Markham's will and my own, of the impossibly numerous sensations and tingling nerve endings and thwarted mating instincts. It couldn't.

"Good," Mr. Markham said, and then he patted my head, stroking my hair softly. "That's a good pet." His words sunk in through my misted mind, strangely soothing. "You want to make me happy, don't you? You want to please your teacher?"

Yes. God yes. I nodded, eagerly this time. Yes, that was what I wanted. For his wide smile to crack that strict expression, for his faint smile lines to crease around those forbidding eyes. I wanted to hear him say that he loved me. I wanted him to praise me.

I was brought over to the sofa, led by my wrists, and then Mr. Markham sat. His shaft was slick and wet and dark now, though I could still see the blue traceworks of his throbbing veins, veins that fed the monster jutting out from his hips. "I'm not going to come in your cunt," he told me. "But you are going to ride me until I am ready to. It is your *task* to make me come." He reached down and cupped his heavy balls, exposed by his open trousers. "I need to come hard, Ivy, do you understand? I need to drain every last drop." He leaned back. "And if you accomplish this task well, you will be rewarded after your punishment."

My cunt pulsed at the thought. Reward. Praise.

Love.

He inclined his head ever so slightly, giving me consent, and I climbed onto him as fervently as a sinner dropping to her knees in church. My tied wrists made it difficult to position myself, and he didn't help. He rested his arms on the back of the sofa, watching me intently, doing nothing to guide himself inside my soaking wet pussy. Finally, I managed, and I drew in a sharp breath at how good he felt, how good it all felt, and I sank down to the root, wiggling a little to impale myself fully.

"Put your hands behind your head. I want to see those tits bounce."

I did as I was ordered and began rocking myself on his cock, grinding my clit against him, feeling my orgasm pulse back into life in mere seconds—

His hands shot out and lifted me up, until only the head of his cock was still notched in my cleft. "*No*," he admonished me. "Bad girl." He let me sink slowly back down. "Up and down only. You are not to come. You are here to fuck me until I spurt, nothing else."

I knew I was whimpering but my resistance was melting away.

Why fight? Why fight, because when I obeyed, he gave me that look of kingly approval and animal desire, fused into one terrifyingly perfect glance—like he was ready to give me his kingdom and fuck me until I sobbed all at the same moment. No, the fight was fading, leaving nothing left but us, but our true selves and our true souls, and the slick sound of my folds embracing his organ, a sound older than any other human sound.

I put my hands behind my head again and kept moving up and down, my thighs—strong from all of my climbing and running and walking—easily lifting and lowering my body.

"More," he said lazily, leaning his head back. His eyes were hooded. "Faster."

I complied, my breasts bouncing as I slid up and down as fast as I could, root to tip, again and again and again. He closed his eyes. "Good," he said and his voice had a quiet hitch in it, like he couldn't quite control his breath. "Oh, that's very good. You're so wet, Ivy. You're so wet and so warm. I could spend all day fucking you, and I will. Damn it all to hell, I *will* have you any way I want, any time I want."

He was swelling, growing harder, and little growls were

escaping from his throat. He opened his eyes—the man gone, nothing left but the animal, that wild entity that was only unleashed when he was deep within me. He looked down at where we were joined. "Milk me with that cunt," he demanded. His expression grew harsh and needy and cruel and uncontrolled, and I almost came just seeing his face. "Yes, like that. Just like that. Faster. Goddammit, I said *faster!*"

A sharp hiss and then I was thrown unceremoniously off, caught around the waist before I truly fell, and shoved onto the floor, facedown. The rug was the best rug in the house, deeply plush and silky against my cheek, but I didn't have time to think about that. Mr. Markham was on top of me, his wet cock burrowing into my ass. I tensed, wondering if this was it—the thing he'd threatened to do on the road, but then he rocked his hips, his length sliding in between the globes of my bottom, and I realized he was rubbing himself off against the soft skin there, pressing my ass tight around his shaft and pumping relentlessly into the slick, snug channel he'd made for himself.

"Look at yourself," he said. "Letting me hold you down and use you. I can see the head of my dick peeping through your ass cheeks when I thrust. My cock is so wet . . . you drenched me earlier with your pussy. Only whores get wet when men use them, Ivy."

His words should have made me feel debased, devalued, but instead, they had me grinding my mound into the rug, arching my back at the same time, wishing against all logic that his cock would slip and find its way back into me where it belonged. He saw this. "You are so greedy for my cock, wildcat. And you'll get it. Just not yet . . . " his voice trailed off as his thrusts became more irregular and frenzied. "That's it," he said roughly. "You're going to feel me spill onto your empty cleft and you're going to like it. *Fuck.*"

He stopped moving and pushed my cheeks apart, exposing the small, sensitive ring of my anus. He held his cock poised there, not stroking himself, just holding his root and pressing the velvet head against the thin, virgin skin. And then he came with a dangerous noise—a noise that sent a shot of adrenaline through me, because it was raw and powerful and it hinted at dissatisfaction and unfinished business. His cum was hot and thick and still more came as he held his dick against my ass and coated me in himself. I wanted to see it, so awfully did I want to see what we looked like right now: me spread facedown on the carpet, him kneeling above me, one hand holding himself as he jetted cum onto my exposed entrance.

And then he was finished, his breathing the only sound in the room other than the fire, which I belatedly realized was very close to my position on the rug. It was warm, so very warm, and I didn't move even as he stood, which ended up being fortunate for me.

When he spoke, his voice was calm and matter-of-fact. "Now we are truly ready for your punishment, Miss Leavold."

CHAPTER 10

*M*y mind was still foggy and my thoughts were still clouded, and so it took me a minute to find the right words and say them coherently. "That wasn't . . . we're still . . . we're not finished yet?"

His low chuckle was silken and lush, and I shivered just hearing it. "I still plan on keeping my promise," he said. "First, I need you to stay exactly where you are. But cross your legs at the ankles."

I complied, feeling the copious wetness he had left on my skin as I did.

"Good." He squatted down by my head, reaching over to plump my bottom. "What do you know about anal sex, Miss Leavold?"

What did he think? I'd been a virgin when I met him. "Nothing. Obviously."

That earned me a hard slap on the flank. "Don't get smart. Answer the question."

I closed my eyes, feeling at sea with this new turn. "I don't know anything about it, Mr. Markham. I know nothing at all."

"Good. I like teaching you. And the first thing to know about anal sex is that you need lubrication. Lots of lubrication. Other-wise, it may hurt you."

I opened my eyes, the word *hurt* sending alarm pinging anew through me.

"I see you're taking my meaning. Good." The hand returned to plumping and caressing, and I sighed despite myself, my uneasiness immediately relaxing under his touch. "There are oils made for such a purpose, oils that can be scented or made to increase sensitivity or made to induce numbness or any other variety of things." His other hand started stroking my hair. "I own all of them. And next time we do this, we will use them. I will make your ass so slippery that sliding into it will be as easy as sliding into your cunt. And I promise that when I fuck you there, you will come, perhaps harder than you ever have before."

Another slap. I jumped involuntarily and his hand was caressing and gentle again, easing me back into relaxation. "But this isn't only about pleasure today. This is about your actions and my discipline. I intend to mark you and make you my own. Make you completely my own, and you will learn that your ass belongs only to me, same as your cunt and your mouth. Is that clear?"

"Yes, Mr. Markham."

"Good girl." He stood. "Today, the only lubrication you get will be from me. From what I just left on you. I hope your ankles are crossed tight, wildcat, because every drop that you let drip down that perfect pussy and onto the floor is one less drop for me to use when I take your ass. And I'm taking it no matter how ready or prepared it is."

I whimpered, afraid again. All of a sudden, I was painfully aware of how his cum was sliding away from where I needed it. I crossed my ankles as tightly as I could, pressing my knees together, trying to hold his essence where it belonged, but the curve of my body made it difficult. I squirmed up, pushing my ass into the air and making my back as concave as possible.

"Please," I said into the carpet. "Please do it now."

"I could," he mused. "I am already hard again. Look at my cock, Ivy."

I looked. His cock was indeed hard again, bobbing slightly as it pulsed thicker and thicker. I swallowed, lust overriding everything else. I wanted him inside so badly.

He walked around my prone form on the floor, absentmindedly massaging himself as he observed me. "You look amazing like this," he said after a minute. "Back arched, dripping with my seed, begging me to take your ass. *This*, my future wife, *this* is the benefit of a good education."

I was shaking now, with combined terror and lust, with my suppressed orgasm and with the effort to keep my body curved upwards. "You'll need to relax," he instructed. "If you relax when I push in, it will hurt so much less. Feel the fire on your body. Feel how it warms your skin and loosens your muscles. Imagine your entire body, from the crown of your head to the tips of your toes, filled with the warmth of the summer sun. Imagine yourself stretched out under that sun like a cat, basking and purring."

I was being petted again, his hands skimming my back and rubbing the outsides of my legs. I did as he said, and I imagined it all, the warmth, the looseness, the catlike desire to be languorous and fluid.

"What a good kitten," he murmured. "Oh, such a good kitten."

I even felt like purring under his expert hands and his husky praise. I tilted my head into his hand when it came there, resting it against his palm. An arm wrapped around my waist as he knelt down beside me again. He pressed a kiss to the back of my neck. "You are perfect," he whispered. "Remember that, because this next part will not be easy for you."

The arm lifted me to my elbows and knees. I was trembling again as he took his place behind me and slid his shaft into my sex. I relaxed an infinitesimal amount, as if I'd been granted a reprieve, but then I felt his finger gently probe the tight ring above my cunt, glazing every secret pleat and crimp with the wetness I'd so anxiously tried to conserve. The finger pushed in easily, and I groaned, feeling nothing but pleasure as I pushed back into him, wanting more of his cock and his finger.

There was that low, silky chuckle again. And then another finger, which I didn't buck into. I stopped, trying to adjust to the new feeling of fullness. The fingers were not still, but rather constantly in motion, moving in and out or tugging experimentally outwards, as if trying to widen the entrance bit by bit. The tugs made me tense, but then Mr. Markham found my clitoris with his other hand and began working it in expert circles. I moaned, pushing back against him then, his fingers no longer a distraction, but a darkly deep bliss.

"That's it," he crooned in my ear. "Good."

And then—just as I was feeling that tension string through my pelvis once more—his fingers were gone.

"I will be honest with you," Mr. Markham said. "I'm not planning on doing this gently. I'm going to fuck your ass as hard as I can. But I promise you that I will finally let you come. In fact, I will *make* you come. Do you trust that I will?"

Why was it that this particular act, more than anything else we'd done, seemed to require so much trust? Why did it seem like such a barrier? But I did trust him, and it was time for me to show it. I let my head drop as I felt him press against my anus.

"I trust you," I said.

And without any further interlocution, he pushed his dick so far up my ass that I cried out. He didn't gentle me or pet me like he had before, he didn't tell me to be quiet, but he did grab hold of my waist with both hands as I tried to squirm away. My mind had gone blank, my lust had evaporated, and all there could be was pain and invasion and the urge to flee.

Flee.

And then, out of nowhere: *Bluebell.*

Bluebell to make it stop, to make the pain stop. But I couldn't even speak; my breath had been driven from my chest, every part of my throat and mouth felt closed and suffocated, yet I was gasping for air, for relief.

And Julian was fucking me all the while, fucking me so hard that his balls slapped against my sex every time he drove himself home. "Ivy, you are so goddamned tight," he said over my whimpers and shrieks. "I wish you could see this, how your tight ass is gripping my cock as if it doesn't want to let it go."

I was still trying to squirm away, and he was still restraining me as he plunged mercilessly into me, and then he said, "You're crying," and I realized I was. I was sobbing, with shuddering breaths and thick tears and no coherent or conscious thoughts in my mind.

"Who is your teacher, Ivy Leavold?"

The words came even though I could barely breathe. "You are."

"And do we leave our teachers? Do we walk away from them without so much as a goodbye?"

The tears were dripping fast and wet onto the rug now, and my chin was quivering. I shook my head.

Mr. Markham stabbed into me with a movement so brutal that I cried out again. "I didn't hear you. Do we walk away from the one person who loves us most in this world *without even a goodbye?*"

"No!" I cried out.

"And why not?"

I shook my head. It was too much. I couldn't think, I couldn't move, I couldn't even breathe.

Another pitiless thrust. "I said, *why not?*"

"Because . . . because you love me."

"Almost. Try again."

God, he was so deep. So deep in such a virgin part of me. And the pain—I found to my shock that it wasn't quite pain anymore, although it wasn't pleasure either. It was sensation, pure and simple, a stimulus that sent electricity to every nerve ending I had—even ones I'd never felt before. Something was kindling besides pain, something so primal, so strange and yet so familiar, and I couldn't name it.

"Try again." His voice was a little softer now, though his motions were not.

"Because," I gasped. "Because I love you. Because I need you. Oh God, Julian, it hurts and it's such a different hurt than I've ever felt, please, please stop."

He slowed and then stopped, his dick still buried completely in my ass. He curved his body over mine. "Say it again."

"Please stop?"

I felt him shake his head. "You know I won't stop unless you use our signal. No, the other thing you said. Say it again, sweetheart."

Sweetheart. I felt a fresh wave of tears at that. He had never used such a tender word with me, not once in our affair. "I love you," I repeated. "And I need you, Julian. I need you always."

He pressed his lips to the curve of my shoulder. And then stopped kissing me and simply rested his face there, breathing in the smell of my skin. "When I saw the ring on the table in your room, I thought my life had ended," he said, and there was no trace of cruelty or anger in his voice, only a tangible, strangled pain. "I know that I must not cage you, but you must promise not to abandon me. If you need to leave, then you must at least give me a goodbye."

I won't leave. But I didn't say the words out loud, because even now, I couldn't be sure that they were true. "I don't want to leave you again," I said instead.

"You are still crying, my love."

"It hurts."

"I know. But you haven't given our signal yet, which tells me that you still want me to teach you this lesson. And you've been such a good pupil, Ivy, so obedient and so willing. Will you trust me a little bit longer?"

After a moment, I nodded slowly. The pain was slowly ebbing away the longer he stayed still, allowing that simmering sensation—the one I couldn't name—to rise to a slow boil. I realized that my nipples were tight and hard, that wetness was dripping from my cunt.

"I want you to relax again. Be my wildcat, be my kitten. Purr and arch and let me pet you. Give yourself entirely over to me right now. Yes, out in the world and in our marriage, you are your own woman, and I would not have it any other way. But in our bed, you are *mine*; your thoughts, your actions, your gasps, and your moans. They are all mine, and I would not have *that* any other way."

His words rolled over me, reassuring in their security, in the safety they represented. The safety I hadn't known until today that I needed.

"Yes," I assented, and I relaxed, feeling everything in me loosen and sigh with relief. "Julian?"

His hands tightened around me at the sound of his name. "Yes, wildcat?" His voice was husky and deep, and he sounded near tears.

"I am yours. Take me."

He held me with his strong arms as he rocked back, so that he was sitting on his heels and I was sitting on him, facing the fire, his cock still deep within me. His fingers found my lower lips and then delved in, curling up as his palm ground against my clit. I melted into him, the pleasure making me loosen, and he slid the tiniest fraction deeper into me.

"That's it," he coaxed. "Good. Now I'm going to set you down and start fucking you again. And you have my permission to come."

He eased me forward and then helped me turn, so that I lay spread on my back. He slowly stroked in and out of me as he gently rubbed my clitoris, and the first jolt of true pleasure made me cry out.

"What is it?" he asked kindly.

"It . . . " I could barely speak, for that dark simmer had now erupted into something more intense than I'd ever felt before. "It feels good."

"It's going to feel even better when you come with my cock in your ass," he promised. "Just stay with me. Feel me."

And I did feel him, every single inch of him, as he pulled out and pushed in. I was panting now, the past hour of denial catching up with me, my body demanding to orgasm even with this new type of pleasure that so closely resembled pain. Mr. Markham grabbed my bound hands and guided them to my swollen center, pressing my fingertips to my bud. "Rub yourself," he commanded, and then he plunged two fingers into my cunt. I did as he ordered, watching his eyes grow darker and darker as he watched me—breasts moving, tied hands pleasuring myself, his shaft pistoning in and out of my virgin ass.

"Keep rubbing," he said, and then used both hands to take my hips. He began pounding hard and deep, but instead of crying out, I grunted and moaned like an animal, feeling a deep surge of pleasure every time he slammed himself home. My hands worked faster and faster on my clit, and then, on a particularly deep thrust, I felt my orgasm coalesce, a looming shape gathering form and strength. It would pull me under, I knew, and I resisted it, twisting sideways and pulling my hands up to my chest.

"Oh no you don't," Julian growled, pressing my shoulder back into the rug. "I'm taking you with me."

He pressed close enough so that the hard muscle above his cock rubbed against my center, and he fucked me with short, fast thrusts that kneaded my clitoris while his cock stroked my ass. I was writhing uncontrollably now, and I no longer knew if I was writhing away or toward him, only that there was nothing left but the fire he had lit and continued to stoke, and everything in me felt so deliciously wound up, so deliciously *full* and *hot*, and I was going to come *so hard*.

"That's a good pet," Mr. Markham said, still growling. "Come for me, sweetheart. I want to watch that pussy clench while I spill into your ass."

It came like a storm—like a hurricane—an unstoppable and devastating force of nature that could not be stayed or diminished. His words removed the last line of resistance, and with a flutter, my clit spasmed, and then my core clenched and released, and then wave after perfect, impossible wave roared through me. I was crying or I was screaming—I was too far gone to know which—but as I rode out the fury of my climax, I saw the naked lust in Julian's eyes as he watched my cunt, watched it pulse and weep. He drove in hard and harder and even harder, until there was no knowing where he ended and I began. And with deep long pulses, he jetted hot bursts of cum into me, pressing in and grinding his dick into my channel with a primitive, cruel strength.

It took minutes for my orgasm to fade, or perhaps it was hours, but when I came to, the fire was still popping merrily on the andiron and I was on Mr. Markham's bare chest, wrapped securely in his arms.

"Give me your left hand, wildcat."

I obeyed, every muscle limp and sated. I felt the cool metal of my engagement ring slide over my knuckles, and I sighed in pure contentment.

"There." His voice was a deep rumble below my ear. "You are mine again, are you not?"

I nodded. I was irrevocably his, every square inch of me, no matter how hidden.

"And I am yours, Ivy. If only you knew how much I am yours."

I nuzzled my face into his chest and let sleep drift over me, not realizing until I was almost past the threshold of unconsciousness that he was saying my name, over and over again, like a man chanting a prayer.

Ivy. Ivy. Ivy.

CHAPTER 11

I hadn't realized I'd been asleep until I awoke.

Strong fingers were rubbing my back, my shoulders, my thighs, massaging a warm oil into my skin and kneading my sore muscles. My eyelashes fluttered open, making a soft whispering noise against the bedsheets. I was on my stomach in Mr. Markham's bed, and everything I could feel ached—ached in a way that was so delicious and satisfying that it barely hurt at all.

"Keep resting, wildcat," Mr. Markham said, his hands now on my calves. "Let me take care of you."

"You already have," I murmured into the bed, fighting the heaviness of sleep to stay awake. The clock on the mantelpiece indicated that it was late evening; I'd been asleep for a few hours at least. "Let me take care of *you* again."

I could almost hear the smile that I knew had to be on his face. "I know you want to. But I would also be a very bad teacher if I didn't help my student recover from her lesson. Now this will hurt for just a moment, but then I promise it will make much of your pain go away."

And then I felt his fingers trail down my back, tracing the line of my tailbone as it curved into my ass and the sore, soft flesh between my legs. I tried to stir, my body shying away, but he kept one hand on my back. "Stay still for a moment," he said, authority coloring his words. I stayed, but I couldn't help squeezing my eyes shut as I felt more oil—a different kind, gauging by the temperature—slide down my skin. And then a single finger pressed against the tight entrance of my ass, pushing in slowly but forcefully. My breath caught—it *hurt*—and I tried not to cry out.

"*Shh*," Mr. Markham soothed, the hand on my back now gentling me, like I was a skittish horse. "*Shh*. Let me take care of you."

The finger worked in and out of me, and it was only after a minute or two of the tear-inducing pain that I realized he wasn't getting ready to fuck me again. He was coating me with oil, inside and out.

"This will numb the pain significantly," he said. "I promise."

And he was right. Within a handful of minutes, the raw pain faded, replaced with a tingling warmth.

"Better?" he asked, climbing off the bed to wash his hands in the nearby basin.

"Much," I said.

When he came back to me, he held a small glass of a reddish-brown liquid. He helped me sit up and bade me to drink it, which I did, although it tasted terrible. He gave me cold water to wash the bitter taste out of my mouth.

"Have you ever had laudanum?"

I shook my head.

He seemed a little surprised. "It will dull the pain and help you sleep, but it may make you sleep very deeply or with very vivid dreams. Don't be frightened if that's the case—I will be here with you." He helped me settle back into the bed. "I must leave you for a time—I am expecting a visitor—but once I finish speaking with him, I promise I will be with you for the rest of the night." He swept a tender kiss across my cheek and then left.

I wished he would stay, but at the same time, I was happy to have a moment to myself, not because I wanted to be away from him necessarily, but because I still needed to process the events of today. The running, the catching, the fucking. All of it, so full of love and turmoil and pain.

Had I known that Mr. Markham could be so barbaric? Surely I had—there was nothing about anything he did that led me to believe he was a gentle soul, deep down. But I would be lying to myself if I didn't admit that I had been genuinely frightened of him, genuinely trying to get away, mere seconds away from uttering our signal. He had hurt me—on purpose—had punished me and had been aroused by doing so. No gentleman did that. No gentleman grew rigid and thick at the thought of a woman sobbing underneath him.

But Mr. Markham did.

I rolled onto my side, watching the fire, feeling the pleasant burn of laudanum pumping through my veins, feeling the sweet ache in my pussy and the tingling numbness of other recovering parts. Why wasn't I running away then? Why hadn't I told him right after that it had been too much, too painful, and that I was leaving? Why did I want it to happen again?

Did that mean something was wrong with me? Was I the truly twisted one in our engagement?

The thought followed me as I spiraled down into sleep. The sleep was as thick as marsh mud, a gloppy clinging sleep that made me wakeful and fretful and sweaty. I twisted in the bed, sweet dreams of kisses and clouds morphing into visions of a frozen field, of Mr. Markham laughing over Violet's corpse. Visions of him fucking her as violently as he had fucked me, visions of him fucking Molly, of him fucking Brightmore. *It's not real*, I would manage to think as I clawed my way back to consciousness, but then I would tumble right back down into the nightmares.

I dreamed I was in a cage, a circus cage, the walls made of iron bars and placed in the middle of a wide tent. There were faces in the crowd, faces I knew—Silas and Molly and Gideon and Helene and the others—and there was a cage next to me. Violet was inside, gripping the bars and staring at me with a tear-streaked face.

Footsteps echoed, boots on the hard-packed dirt of the ground, and Mr. Markham came into view. I could see only his legs, long and firm, and a whip dangling at his side. I knew—somehow—that if I didn't perform, if I was an unsatisfactory pet, that I would feel the whip. I looked at Violet, now sobbing, and I also knew that something worse than punishment might happen. If I disappointed Julian, would I be abandoned? Killed?

Except—how disturbing—there was a part of me that craved this fear. In fact, it barely felt like fear at all because it was so energizing, so electrifying. God, what was wrong with me?

The whip struck the ground and I jumped, starting to shudder with dread and excitement as the keys jingled. I was about to be let out. I would have to perform . . .

I jolted awake, the sheets twisted tightly around me and sweat making my hair stick to my face. Adrenaline spiked my blood and the laudanum made it impossible to think clearly, and I couldn't tell whether the walls were made of stone or iron bars and I could hear the keys still jingling, jangling . . .

But it was the clatter of hooves in the courtyard. Mr. Markham's visitor.

I decided to get up and get a drink, which I did, groggily and shakily, my hands and limbs feeling too weak to hold my glass. *The laudanum.* It worked well. I leaned against the window, resting my tired head against the glass, as a small man with white hair climbed easily off his horse. Nobody came out to greet him, but a rectangle of yellow light cast on the dim driveway told me that the door was opened. The man strode right in, his posture respectable and polite but his steps determined.

It was the man from the hotel in York. The one who had known my name.

I made a decision despite the growing murkiness of my

thoughts, pulling on the scarlet dressing gown and belting it tightly, moving to the door as quietly as I could. A thousand questions raced through my mind. Did Mr. Markham know this man? Had he known him when he'd seen him in York? And how did the man know *me*? And, above all, why hadn't Mr. Markham told me that this visitor was the same person we'd seen in York?

Was he trying to keep it a secret?

But I only made it as far as the door before my knees grew too weak to support my weight. I held on to the door handle for a moment, trying to summon the strength to keep moving, but there was no hope. I'd been given more laudanum than I thought, perhaps, because I could feel the blackness at the edges of my vision, the tumbling of my thoughts growing erratic and dreamy, and I managed to find an armchair nearby before I collapsed and knew no more.

* * *

IT WAS morning when I woke—early morning, gauging by the rosy light filtering in through the curtains. I was no longer in the armchair but in bed, a long, muscled body pressed against mine. I was gathered in his arms, my face to his chest, and I could tell by his breathing that he was awake. Awake and unhappy.

I tilted my head back to look up at him.

"Good morning, wildcat." A small smile curved his lips. "You slept like the dead last night."

It had felt that way, although the lingering tendrils of nightmares still brushed at my mind—leering faces and whispered threats, Mrs. Brightmore's scowl and Mrs. Harold's honeyed voice, Molly's sharp eyes and Julian's rasping words. The prickling feeling of being watched by unseen eyes.

If the dead dreamed, surely those were the kinds of dreams they had.

"What's wrong?" Julian murmured. "Your face—it has gone distant just now."

"Nothing's wrong," I whispered, even though I knew that wasn't quite true. But I wasn't sure what, exactly, was wrong. Save for a feeling. A glimmer of intuition.

He brushed the backs of his fingers across my cheek. "You've gone somewhere in your mind, Ivy. Come back to me."

I took a deep breath and did as he asked, refocusing my thoughts on him and him alone. He lowered his lips to mine, and I softened into him, letting his breath entwine with my own, molding my curves as tightly as I could against the lean lines of his body.

He pulled back. "You were such a good pet last night," he said, his concerned murmur slowly changing back to his usual commanding tone. "You let me fuck you so hard. And you liked it, didn't you? You liked it when I took your ass. You came so beautifully, wildcat. I could feel every squeeze and flutter of your perfect body."

I nodded, pressing my head against his chest once more, feeling my breathing start to speed up. My dreams came back to me, the sneaking fear that someday I wouldn't be able to perform, that I wouldn't be able to be the good pet he wanted. And with it came the twisted longing to be totally at one with him, even his darkness. Especially his darkness.

"And now I will reward you," he said. "You deserve to be spoiled."

Anticipation started to stir in my belly. "How will you reward me?"

"You choose."

"Then I want you to fuck me," I said without hesitation. I had none of these bothersome worries and anxieties when he was inside me. When we were together, our union felt so safe, indissoluble.

He laughed to himself. "I know, but that's not how this works. Today, I want you to do whatever you want with me. Today, I want you to take your pleasure selfishly. Use me however you like, because today, my mouth and cock and fingers belong only to you."

I bit my lip, confusion warring with my growing desire. He'd always been the dominant force in our affair, the one who shaped and directed our encounters, the one who determined when and how my orgasms would come. It was an alien feeling, being in control in bed. But my slowly throbbing clit and tightening nipples were not about to complain. I blinked away the last of my laudanum grogginess and then pushed him onto his back. The sheets pulled away from his shirtless body and I could see how hard he was in his trousers, a rigid outline that was mine to explore and use today.

But I was sore—deeply sore—and I knew I would need to be ready for him. So instead of climbing on top of him, I positioned myself above his shoulders on my knees, so that my bare cunt was a mere inch from his face.

"*Yes*," he groaned, not waiting for me to lower myself, but instead raising up and capturing my sensitive flesh with his mouth, sucking and nibbling at turns. His tongue flicked over my clit, lightly at first, before moving to lick at my hole, plunging in and out. After the exhaustion of last night and with the honeyed influence of the opium still fogging me, I couldn't support myself much longer, and my knees slid down so that I was now riding his face. I tried to raise myself back up, certain that he was uncomfortable, but he wrapped his arms around my thighs, trapping me to his face as he fucked me with his tongue.

He made noises of deep satisfaction, noises of deep hunger, as if this were the only thing he ever wanted to do, and it was those noises—and the very prominent display of arousal behind me—that sent me over the edge. I bucked shamelessly against his face, forgetting about his comfort, forgetting about dignity, just riding his mouth as I quivered and clenched and panted, riding his face so hard that I could feel his stubbled chin grating across my flesh.

I slowly stilled, looking down into his aventurine eyes as I did, leaning back so that my weight rested on his chest instead of his face.

"Oh wildcat," he breathed. "You don't know how difficult it is not to flip you over and fuck you right now. Just tasting you makes me hard. But having you take my mouth like that makes me dangerous."

He wasn't lying. His eyes blazed and his body trembled ever so slightly, as if he were fighting to restrain himself. I slid off him and then off the bed, indicating with a gesture that I wanted him to stay there. I wanted to look at him for a moment. At the expensive trousers tented by his cock and at the sharply muscled lines of his stomach, with that line of dark hair that led from his navel down past the waistband of his pants. His lips still wet from me.

"You look a little wild right now, Ivy. What are you thinking about? Do you want to ride my face again? Or would you like to sink onto my cock and ride me that way? I know that beautiful cunt will be hungry until it's filled. How will you let me fill it?"

I stepped forward and tugged down his trousers. "Quiet," I told him. "You're distracting me."

He grinned, grinned like a man getting his pants taken off by a naked woman. "Good."

I climbed back on the bed and straddled him. "I'm going to fuck you until I come," I told him. "But this time, you aren't allowed to come until *I* say."

His smile faded, a dark and brutal look replacing it. "Do you think that's wise, wildcat?"

"You said this was my reward, that I could do with you as I wish." I slid my wet cunt along the underside of his shaft, which earned me a low hiss. "I'm choosing to use you. I'm going to use this thick cock to come, and then maybe I'll think about letting you climax too."

And with that, I guided his dick into my cleft, sinking down and groaning softly. Despite the delicious orgasm I'd just had, I was still very sore from last night and there was a sting of pain raking along my pleasure, pain from the rough fucking he'd given my pussy and also from the pressure this position exerted on the other part he'd fucked.

He moved his hips underneath me, and I slapped his chest. "Stop it," I said. "Stay still."

He didn't look happy, but he obeyed. I took advantage of this and began rocking myself against him, not moving up and down, but grinding my clit against him as hard as I could, moving faster and faster. I could see the muscles jumping and twitching in Mr. Markham's arms and chest as he fought himself from grabbing me and fucking me on his own terms. It was so deliciously foreign, having control, and I felt almost giddy as I ground down harder and faster, reaching up with both hands to hold my sweaty hair off my neck, which lifted my tits higher. His gaze was glued to them as I moved, as I became less graceful and more ferocious with my movements, my thoughts dying away as some primal part of me took over. There was only the building tightness low in my belly, only his thick cock spurring me on towards an encroaching summit.

"That's it," he growled. "Come, kitten. Come on me. Let me see how much you love my cock."

I did love it and I did come, slow spasms of pleasure gathering and gathering as I bore down on his thick member, impaled myself on it like I had nothing else to live for, like there was nothing else but this perfect part of this perfect person whom I loved.

And then, like a firework, I ignited. Caught fire and blew up in explosions of red and blue and gold, crying out as my womb clenched and squeezed around him.

He waited—impatient and hungry but still as a statue—as I rode out my pleasure on him, rode it hard and heedlessly, not caring what I looked like or sounded like. I slowly slumped forward, half lying on his chest with my face near his ear, his stone-hard organ still buried inside me.

His voice was low. "Wildcat. I'm feeling quite vicious at the moment. Are you going to let me come?"

"I want to see it," I said, moving off him.

"What?"

"I want to see you come. I want to see you fill me with it."

His cock throbbed. "Is that so?"

There was a mirror attached to the table that held his water ewer and basin. I moved a chair in front of the mirror and then angled the mirror to the side so that I would be able to see its reflection if someone were in front of me. I sat on the edge of the chair and spread my legs. "Come here."

He was there in a moment, his hair tousled and his manhood almost painfully veined and purpled as he knelt in between my legs.

"Put it inside of me," I ordered.

"Christ," he muttered and closed his eyes. "I can't—when you talk like that—" He gripped my thighs, not moving. "I almost come when you say things like that."

"I don't care," I told him honestly. "Do what I tell you."

His jaw clenched and his eyes burned with something that looked very close to anger, and then he stabbed inside of me with one brutal stroke. I arched my back and whimpered with delight, with need. He stayed inside for a moment, waiting for my next command.

"Make yourself come," I said breathlessly. "But come hard. I want to see it spilling out of me."

"Shit," he swore, drawing himself out and then slamming back into me. Ruthless thrusts, barbaric thrusts, and God, nothing had ever felt better. Each slam pounded against my clitoris and each stroke dragged his wide crown against something inside that made me toes curl.

"Are you going to come again?" he asked, still pounding into me. "You like it when you're fucked hard? You need it, don't you? You need to be fucked by me all the time. Such a naughty kitten, needing to come so much."

My fingernails were scratching his neck now, his shoulders and his chest, not in protest but in the helpless animalism he always brought out in me.

"I'm going to . . . " Even if I could have breathed, I wouldn't have been able to finish my sentence, I was so far gone.

"Watch," he said. "This is what you wanted, right? You wanted to see yourself filled up with cum. So look, wildcat, because I'm going fill you full of it."

He used one hand to grip my jaw and turn my gaze to the mirror, which showed me his tight ass pumping between my legs. I pulled my legs up, bracing my feet on the edge of the chair and exposing my pussy. Mr. Markham didn't miss a single thrust, didn't adjust his rhythm in the slightest. He kept fucking me, and now I could properly see the wide, slick cock pushing in and out of my pink folds.

"Here it comes," he growled, and then his thrusts went long and violent, his head dropping as he rammed into me. I watched in the mirror, entranced at how my body responded to him, the way my cunt welcomed him to the root even as I could see his full load beginning to spill out of me. He grunted and shuddered, finally looking down at where we were joined, swallowing hard as he saw his seed dripping free.

"Did you like that?" he asked, reaching between us to stroke my clit. My orgasm—held temporarily at bay by my fascination —began to surge forward again and I rocked against his hand and his still-hard penis. "Do you like it when I come inside of you?"

I nodded, unable to speak.

"Good," he said, his voice possessive and uncivilized. "Because I'm going to fill you up every day for the rest of your life."

And then I exploded once again, filled with him, held by him, every part of me his, and yet still I wanted more.

CHAPTER 12

*R*ain was supposed to be bad luck on a wedding day.

I thought about this as I paced in my room, clad in a white and gold dress that cost more than most people made in a single year. It had elbow-length sleeves and a high collar in back, a collar that plunged into a low neckline in front—daring for a morning wedding, but Mr. Markham had wanted the design and I frankly didn't care. And a secret part of me had to admit it was delightful to wear such a beautiful dress. It sparkled and glinted and rustled, the thick drapes and folds of the skirt making me feel like a princess out of a long-ago tale.

Of course, no princess had an attendant quite as annoying as I'd managed to acquire. Mrs. Harold, the rector's wife, had shown up this morning, fluttering her eyelashes and telling me how she just *knew* I wouldn't have anyone to help me get ready and how that was such a *crime.*

And what could I do? I didn't have anybody to help me dress, and as tiresome as I found her, I did need the help with the elaborate gown and with my hair.

"You look like a *vision,*" she told me, handing me a lacy gold shawl to drape from my elbows. "Mr. Markham will be so taken."

"*Mm.*" It was hard to focus, hard to concentrate. Today was so permanent, so final, and it felt strange to make such a move when I still felt uncertain about so much. I watched Mrs. Harold's cerulean dress swirl around her feet as she went back to the chair she'd been sitting on. She had long feet for such a slender woman.

"He's a difficult man to please," Mrs. Harold said. "Aren't you worried about what your marriage will be like?"

I was still staring at the hem of her dress, swaying and lifting as she sat, her pointed shoes exposed. "No," I said distractedly. "I'm not worried." Something was fitting itself together in my mind, something she had told me weeks ago. And I was an idiot for not seeing it before.

"Mrs. Harold?" I asked. "Didn't you tell me that you had heard about Mr. Markham laughing when he found Violet's body?"

She blinked at the abruptness of the question, and I watched with interest as her eyes slid away from my face to the corner of the room. "Yes," she said. "Yes, the servants saw it. But my dear, isn't it a little *late* to be worrying about all this? You're due at the church in an hour."

"But the servants didn't see it." I stepped closer to her, her position on the chair creating a height difference that obviously made her uncomfortable. I stared down at her, at her pretty if sharp features. "*You* saw it, didn't you? It was you at the edge of the field. Your footprints in the frost."

She opened her mouth and then closed it. Mrs. Harold, at a loss for words. But I didn't have time to marvel. "I saw the sketches of the footprints at the police station," I told her. "The feet so large they suspected they belonged to a man. But they belonged to you, didn't they? The question is, why were you there? And why did you lie?"

She stood suddenly, her face white and pinched. "You listen to me," she hissed. "You are about to marry a dangerous man.

You have no idea the things he's done, the things he's willing to do—he is beyond vicious. He is *evil*."

She took a breath. "Yes, I was there," she finally admitted. "I was leaving the house early, and I saw him walking out from the stables. At first, I thought he was looking for Violet—he was calling her name and running, but then I knew that he must have known what happened, because he ran straight for where Raven was standing. Straight for where Violet's body was. And there was no way I would tell him I saw—I knew how violent he was. Who knows what he would have done to me?" Her voice was high-pitched and strange, and there was more than fear in it, there was *experience*, somehow.

I had to know. "Did he really laugh?"

"No." Her eyes met mine. "He howled. Like a beast."

"So you lied." I don't know why I was angry that the town gossip had lied—it was like being angry that a hawk had eaten a rabbit. But still, on Julian's behalf, I felt furious.

Her chin tipped upward defiantly. "The essence of it is true— he didn't care that Violet had died. He *wanted* to hurt her. You have no idea how much he wanted her to suffer. He loved it when she cried. When she begged. His howl could have been a howl of victory, not of grief."

"You don't know these things," I said. "How could you?"

"Oh, I *know*." And for some reason, she was crying now. "And you do too. Let me ask you, Miss Leavold, has he ever treated you in a way that society would consider unacceptable? Has he ever made you afraid? Has he ever shown desire at the sight of your fear?"

"I—" Yes. The answer was yes. But I couldn't answer.

"Congratulations on your nuptials, Miss Leavold. You are marrying a monster, and what's worse, you're doing it knowing full well that you've been warned. Don't expect me to come to your funeral too."

I was the one who sat now, unable to speak, as Mrs. Harold left without saying a goodbye.

* * *

THIRTY MINUTES LATER, and I was waiting for Gareth to pull the carriage around for me so I could join my future husband at the church. My hands were shaking. Shaking hard.

Was I ready for this? Could I be ready for this? Mrs. Harold had shaken me deeply. *Has he ever shown desire at the sight of your fear?*

Yes.

But I had also felt desire in conjunction with my fear, so what did that make me? Was I a monster like he was? He was no gentleman, but I was no lady. Ladies didn't crave the things I craved.

No. I had made my choice three weeks ago in the lane to Stokeleigh. I'd decided to stay, decided to trust that I was safe. Decided to trust that whatever had happened the night Violet died, Mr. Markham at least hadn't been the one to directly take her life. And that had to count for something, a small weight to bear against my ever-present doubts.

Besides, I thought as I turned and made my way downstairs, *Mr. Markham has shown me nothing but passion, love, devotion, generosity, and domination.* All things I needed. He'd taken me into his home, into his bed, protected me, and was even trying to make an honorable woman out of me by offering his hand in marriage. There was nothing about him in our time together that indicated he would hurt me, at least not in a way I didn't want. He had even promised to tell me the truth—and let me leave if that truth became too much.

Yes. I am sure this is what I want.

I descended the stairs into the foyer, where the front doors were already open and waiting, revealing the thundering sky and the sheets of silver-gray rain. I thought I could hear the sounds of the carriage coming up from the stables, but it was impossible to tell over the low rumble of the storm.

"Miss Leavold."

I started, surprised to see the white-haired man from York. He'd been standing in the doorway to the parlor, concealed by the rainy morning shadows, but the fresh drops on his jacket indicated that he hadn't been inside long.

"You," I said. "You came here a few weeks ago."

He inclined his head politely, agreeing. "It is interesting you know that, Miss Leavold. I was under the impression you were out visiting with friends at the time. I had insisted on coming here to visit you myself, and then conveniently you were not at home."

I paused. I couldn't puzzle the right information out of his words.

He seemed to understand this. He reached into his pocket and withdrew a small white card.

Jonathan Wright, Esq.

33 Portage Street, York

"I'm an old friend of Edward Wickes," he said. "We studied law together, and we now frequently assist each other when the need arises. For example, when trying to hunt down a certain young woman known to live at Markham Hall."

My confusion was not abated at all. "Why would Solicitor Wickes be looking for me? And why send you to come talk to me—why not simply write?"

"He did write, Miss Leavold. He's been writing you for almost three months now. And you haven't answered a single letter. The situation was important enough that he felt it required a more dramatic intervention. So he called upon me."

"He hasn't written," I said. "Or the letters got sent to the wrong address. Or—"

"Or," he said softly, "somebody's been taking them before you could read them."

"But who—" No. It was ridiculous. None of the servants cared enough about me to steal my mail, and while Mrs. Bright-more hated me, I couldn't picture her confiscating letters. Surely not.

Right?

"Whatever the case may be, I am here to deliver two messages. One is that Mr. Wickes is very anxious to see you, but his health makes it impossible for him to leave London at present. He is hoping that you will visit him as soon as you can arrange for a visit. He has even offered to pay for the trip himself, if you need him to."

I shook my head, still feeling confused. "No, that won't be necessary," I said. "I'll be traveling to London today actually. We leave this afternoon."

Mr. Wright looked over my dress, the small white rosebuds in my hair. "After your wedding," he said.

"Yes."

He glanced at the floor a moment, and in that moment, I saw that he made a decision, swallowing back something with visible effort.

"The second message Mr. Wickes wants to convey is that you yet have a relative living. Your aunt, Esther Leavold. She is lately returned from India and was most horrified to learn of your circumstances. She wishes to be reunited with you at once, and she wants you to know that you are invited to come live with her." He looked at my dress again. "Although it has only been since today that I understood Mr. Markham's intentions for you. I am afraid your aunt and Mr. Wickes have no idea that your situation is changing so drastically."

His words were not filtering in properly, not finding residence in anything I was prepared to understand. I felt the need to sit immediately, and he sensed this, taking my elbow and guiding me to a low ancient bench. I sat, my head feeling light.

"My aunt? But she never wrote back when we tried to reach her, and there was talk that she must have died..." My voice broke on this last word, broke hard, and I felt tears pricking at the back of my eyelids. "So I never thought—I mean, I had rather given up on . . . "

I couldn't finish. But I didn't need to. Mr. Wright understood.

I'd been orphaned. I had grieved and accepted that there would be no one out there bound to me by blood, no one who was born with an obligation to love me and care for me. And I had survived the grief. Adapted and grown and against all odds had found a new life for myself here in the north, in Mr. Markham's arms. And now everything had changed in an instant.

"I should go," Mr. Wright said. "I have been given the distinct impression that Mr. Markham does not want me to talk to you."

I looked up, my eyes wet. "You have?"

Mr. Wright knelt in front of me, very easily for a man of his years, and gave me a grave but kind look. "It is not my place to advise you on anything of a personal nature, but I feel compelled to warn you that some perceive Mr. Markham to be a dangerous man."

I was already shaking my head, but he held up a hand. "I know it is not what you want to hear. But have you given any thought as to why Mr. Markham wouldn't want us to communicate? Have you considered that he might have taken Mr. Wickes' letters before you could read them?"

"No," I whispered. "That's not what happened."

"I hope not." He stood. "Congratulations on your upcoming marriage, Miss Leavold. And please make your way to London as quickly as possible."

And he vanished into the rain.

* * *

THE ENCOUNTER HAD LASTED BARELY five minutes. Gareth still wasn't present with the carriage, and I didn't know what to do with myself. I paced up and down the hallway, pausing at the door to the library.

Have you considered that he might have taken Mr. Wickes' letters?

No. They were lost. Sent to the wrong address or mixed up. And so what if Mr. Markham had told Mr. Wright I'd been away that night—I certainly had not been in a state to receive him anyway, not with the amount of laudanum I'd taken.

Not with the amount of laudanum he'd given me.

I was walking in circles before the library door now, the gold silk of my dress brushing against the medieval flags of the entry hall, my new boots clicking impatiently on the floor. An idea formed, a half idea really, the shade of a premise with barely any logic, but it was fed by the undercurrent of doubt that now swelled in my mind. I didn't stop to ponder or pull the idea apart, I simply acted, hurrying up the stairs and going into Mr. Markham's room, empty of its owner but still smelling of grass and summer, of the particular soap he liked to use. I ignored all this, ignored my pounding pulse and the heat behind my eyelids, and I dropped to my knees by his bed.

I gazed for a moment at the trunk underneath, incongruously gleaming in the dusty space under the bed. *AW* sparkled golden, even in the dim light. I reached for it, just barely able to snag the corner with a fingertip. It was heavy, and I had to flatten myself on the floor before I could properly shift it to a place where I could pull it out.

It was a smallish trunk, but solid, and the well-oiled hinges did not creak as I lifted the lid. I expected oft-creased and caressed love letters from years ago, locks of hair and handkerchiefs and pressed flowers. I expected the things that a man would keep to remember a sweet wife who died too young.

There was nothing like that. In fact, the trunk was empty save for eight letters, all addressed to me, all sent from Solicitor Wickes. All opened.

I picked one of them up, hands shaking, and slowly unfolded the paper, reading the cordial missive informing me of my aunt Esther's return to England. The next informing me that she was inviting me to stay with her. The next asking politely if I had received the first two. And so on and so on, each letter growing more worried than the last.

Mr. Markham had read them. Mr. Markham had hidden them.

Why?

"I was planning on showing you the letters," a voice said from behind me. "After the wedding."

I turned, my heart thudding, to see Julian leaning tiredly against the doorway, clad in a sharply pressed morning suit. His wedding suit. I dropped the letters guiltily, like a sinner caught sinning, even as anger flared at the sight of him.

"You're not at the church," I said in a hoarse voice.

"Gareth got me the moment he saw Mr. Wright's horse tied up in front. I came right away. I didn't want him to speak to you. For reasons that are now apparent."

"They aren't apparent," I said, and I realized there was a tremulousness in my voice that edged on hysteria. "They aren't apparent at all. Why are these letters under your bed? Why would you hide the fact that I have a relative? Why, when you knew how desperately I missed having a family?"

He was by me in an instant, on his knees, his face close to mine. "*I* am your family now," he said heatedly. "Me. Only me."

His hand was gripping my upper arm. Hard. "You and my family aren't mutually exclusive," I said. "I can have you both."

"I don't want to share you," he said harshly. "With anyone."

I wrenched away from him. "And why is that? Were you worried that I would leave you if I had another choice? Did you think that I was only marrying you—only fucking you—because I needed a place to live?"

Now he was the one to blanch. "No—"

"Because we've been over that," I said over him. "You knew that wasn't the case. You knew that I loved you for who you *are* —that I would love you even if I was an heiress with millions of pounds to my name. Why couldn't you trust that I would love you no matter what happened?"

He ran a hand through his hair, a shaky, violent motion that betrayed vulnerability and possessiveness and guilt. I stood and turned away so that I wouldn't have to see it.

"Come back here," he snapped. "You don't get to walk away from me."

He stood and grabbed at my arm. I spun around and slapped him. He staggered back.

"You *lied* to me, Julian! Why? *Why?*"

He didn't touch his cheek, even as red splotches bled across his freshly shaven skin. "Ivy," he said in a low voice. "Don't do this. Please."

"You either answer my questions or I leave this room."

We stared at each other for a long moment, and I knew he could see the resolve written across my features. He took a deep breath and finally spoke. "I didn't want you to have the option to leave me. If you found out about the night Violet died, about the things I did. I didn't want it to be easy for you to walk away from me."

I was too strong to buckle or swoon, but I still backed against the dressing table, my fingers wrapping around its edges for support. His answer was so honest—*too honest*—and it was terrifying. He wanted me trapped here. He wanted to make it as hard as it could be for me to leave him, even after he'd promised me that I could leave at any time.

"You said," and now the emotion broke through, shaking my voice and wetting my eyelashes. "You said that I could leave when you told me the truth. Or after you told me. You said I could leave whenever I wanted!"

He was breathing heavily. "I meant it, wildcat—"

"Don't call me that!" I said, suddenly furious. "You don't get to call me that now!"

Anger glittered in his eyes. "I can call you whatever I like. Because you're mine, Ivy. You were mine the moment you let me circle your wrist with my hand the night we met. You were mine from the moment I pulled your first orgasm from your body on the floor of my library. You are mine and I have every right to protect what's mine."

"So I can't leave." My words were flat.

He shook his head, defensively, desperately. "That's not what I'm saying. You can leave. You can utter *bluebell* at any time and I'm at your mercy. I only hid the letters for now because I wanted to show you . . . I wanted to show you how perfect I could make your life if you gave yourself completely to me and became my wife. Then I would tell you about Violet. Then I would tell you about your aunt. But first I needed you to be mine in the eyes of the law and of God. I needed to show you everything I could give you."

It was always going to come to this, I realized. It was always going to come down to his secrets, his mysteries, his guilt. And I loved him with every atom and molecule that vibrated in my body, but I couldn't live with those secrets any longer. I would always love him, always want to be with him, but treachery and betrayal was a line I couldn't force myself to cross.

"Tell me what happened the night she died."

He came to me and circled my upper arms with his hands. "No, Ivy, not yet. Listen to me—"

"Don't touch me."

His hands dropped and he stepped back. "Please," he whispered. "Let me make it right."

"If you want to make it right, then you'll tell me," I cried. "If you didn't kill her, why can't you just tell me?"

"Because I don't want you to hate me," he said. Sadness sliced through his words like broken glass.

"Don't you see that I will anyway? If you try to trap me here? If you keep lying to me?"

"Once you know this, you can't unknow it," he said. "It . . . it's the worst thing I've ever done. The worst thing in a lifetime of bad deeds. Please, Ivy. Please let it go."

I took a step toward the door, unable to wrestle with him any longer. Our signal pressed against the inside of my lips, begging to be uttered. One word and he would have to let me leave.

"Wait," he said. "Please."

I stopped and looked at him, not bothering to wipe the tears from my face. Tears that dripped hot and fast onto my wedding dress.

Mr. Markham sank into a chair, burying his face in his hands. "I fucked someone else."

My stomach rose into my chest, and I knew I was going to be sick. What was he saying? He had been with another woman . . . recently? While he was supposed to be with me?

He couldn't mean that. He wouldn't mean that.

"Julian," I started but then couldn't finish.

"The night Violet died. I fucked another woman." He looked up at me. "You have to understand, fidelity was—is—one of the most important things to me. When my mother was alive, my father never made a secret of his mistresses or the maids he fucked or the houseguests he seduced. Mother never complained, pretended not to notice, but I could see how it killed her inside. So I vowed that I would never do that to someone I loved. To someone I didn't love, even. So when Violet cheated on me with my valet, I was furious. I had suspected something for weeks but hadn't been certain. Didn't want to believe it. And then she told me she was pregnant—" He bit off his own words and stared dully ahead. "I wanted to be a good husband, Ivy. Even after I realized that I didn't love her, that I couldn't be married to her any longer, I wanted to provide for her. Set aside a house and a decent living for her and her child. But she threatened to kill herself when I brought it up. She vacillated between suicide and threatening to fuck my servants and my friends in my own bed. I was infuriated. She stormed out of the house. I decided to give her time to cool off, then after our guests left, I would bring her back. Talk to her. Silas and I searched, and we couldn't find her. So I sent for the police and decided to catch a couple hours of sleep while we waited for them to arrive."

I slowly sat in a nearby chair. "What happened?"

Old pain flashed in his eyes. "She made good on her promise. I found her fucking Gareth in my bed."

"Oh, Julian."

"I was so angry—livid and furious—I could barely think. I never blamed Gareth, you understand; I'd seen my father threaten and coerce enough servants into having sex with him that I knew it wasn't really Gareth's fault. But I blamed her. Yes, I blamed her."

"What did you do?" My voice was barely audible now.

"At first? Nothing. I stormed out of the hallway and walked right into Brightmore. She had seen everything. She knew everything."

I was beginning to understand. Remembered Brightmore's words. *I told the master how to handle a wayward wife. And he did.*

"She didn't say anything at first. But she left and she came back with the rector's wife. Mrs. Harold had contrived some excuse or another to stay the night, probably for a chance to be alone with me. Our paths had crossed at many social events in the past . . . I knew she wanted me to take her to bed. I'd never followed up on her advances; I was never interested." He sighed. "Brightmore dragged her to me. She told me that I needed to show Violet that I was the husband, I was the master, that her adultery would not be tolerated."

Mrs. Harold. Her tears today made more sense now.

I had a hand pressed to my mouth now, the other hand fisted in my skirts. Oh God, the skirts that Mrs. Harold had helped dress me in . . . for my fucking *wedding*. The woman that Brightmore had hauled before Mr. Markham like a concubine had helped me prepare to marry him, and she had tried to warn me . . .

Julian buried his face in his hands. "And God help me, I listened. I wanted Violet to know—to *feel*—how I felt, even if it was only for a second, even if it was the barest shadow of the feeling. I pulled the rector's wife into my room, threw Gareth out, and rounded on Violet. I tied her wrists to my bedpost."

"What did you do to her?"

"To her? Nothing. But to Mrs. Harold . . . " He trailed off and then gave a bitter laugh, a dark noise that sent chills down my spine. "You know, she didn't even say anything when my house-keeper brought her to me, or when I tied Violet naked and crying to my bed. She dropped to her knees when I told her to, opened her mouth when I told her. All in front of my wife."

I tried to hide the disgust in my voice. "So you made Violet watch?"

He looked at me. "If I'm to make a confession, I should confess it all. I may be damned, wildcat, but for some reason I feel as if we are damned together. That you will love me anyway."

I glanced away from him. He'd hit upon the confusion that had been dogging me these past few weeks, the worry that I was as monstrous and toxic as he was. And he was right, I would love him anyway.

But loving and staying were two different things.

He stood, pacing in a jerky, agitated way. "I know I'm a terrible man, Ivy. But you must understand, I've never been that angry, before or since. All I could think about was hurting Violet in the same way she'd hurt me. The rector's wife was so eager too, even with Violet right there. I fucked her over and over again, on her knees, bent over a chair, on the floor. I fucked her until I got bored with her, with my anger. I fucked her until I got bored of hearing my wife cry.

"I was consumed with watching Violet. I didn't look at Mrs. Harold once. No, I only watched Violet, and the way she watched us. The way she begged me to stop. She tried to look away, but I wouldn't let her. I told her I'd keep her tied to the bed for the rest of the day if she did." He closed his eyes. "I can still hear her now. Sobbing, yelling obscenities."

I lowered my hand, feeling ill. I imagined Violet's tears, her flushed and splotchy face as she demanded to be untied, as she begged Mr. Markham to stop. I'd known he could be barbaric. But this . . .

"It all made me hard. Her futile rage. Her betrayed shock. Her incandescent hatred. No matter how much I came, it wasn't enough to release me from my need for revenge; I was able to fuck that Harold woman over and over again while Violet watched. I was lost to myself," he continued. "But I didn't care. I didn't care at all anymore, and that's what I realized at the end, as she screamed at me, as I fucked another man's wife in front of my own. After a couple hours, I finally sent the woman away and untied Violet, expecting her to hit me, to try to hurt me. I would have let her. I hated her and I hated myself, and for a while revenge felt delicious. But in the end, it was an empty gesture. Nothing would heal us, not punishment, not discipline, not matching betrayal for betrayal."

He sat again, staring at the fire. "She never expected me to fight back like that, I think. She was so used to everybody—lovers and family and friends—giving her everything she wanted. I know that's what broke her."

I was such a tangle of confused feelings at that moment. I was horrified by Mr. Markham's cruelty, terrified that he could wield that same cruelty against me. But I also couldn't deny that there was a certain sickening justice in what he had done.

I couldn't deny that a part of me, low and dark, flickered with something like jealousy of Violet or of Mrs. Harold. I didn't cry when Julian unleashed his worst on me, I climaxed. And then begged for more. What would I have done? What would I have felt?

And why was I even considering something so awful?

"But she didn't fight me. She'd stopped screaming by that point and was just staring at me. I'd never seen her like that . . . so upset and yet so quiet." He ran his hands through his hair. "I told her to leave—that I planned on riding to Scarborough myself to tell the police she'd been found and that a formal search would be unnecessary. She didn't storm away, she didn't yell. She left. But I could see it in her—in the way her face had gone white, in the way her hands shook. She was about to break. Violet never bore anything patiently or quietly. This was the calm before the storm."

"And then she died."

"And then she died," he echoed hollowly. "She'd always been a horsewoman, and she rode whenever she was upset or angry or happy . . . anything she felt, really, was reason to ride. When I got to the stables to leave for Scarborough and I saw Raven missing, I knew." His voice cracked. "I knew she'd taken him. Of course, she was such a good rider, I didn't worry. Not at first."

The fire popped and I closed my eyes, still fighting back nausea. The rain outside continued to lash at the windows, thunder rolled in from distant skies, and the wind tossed the leafy branches and blew around the old corners of the hall. I listened to the comforting sounds of the storm, wishing I was outside running in it. Wishing I was away from this truth and this man. This cruel, perfect man.

"I didn't cut the saddle," Mr. Markham said quietly, his voice barely audible over the rain. "But I was the reason she climbed into it in the first place."

CHAPTER 13

I could find no words to convey the tangled feelings and thoughts inside of me. I couldn't even look at him right then.

He had been right. It was a truth I didn't want to know now that I knew it. It did make me despise him. And I despised him all the more because he had hidden it for so long, trapping me with my own ignorance. But at the same time, I felt a relief so palpable and distinct, it was almost painful. He hadn't murdered Violet. He wasn't going to murder me.

My life was safe with him.

But I was also more than animated flesh—I was a soul, a mind, a creature of love and feeling. Would all that be safe with Julian Markham?

Only one thing was clear to me in that moment: I had to go. I had to leave Markham Hall, perhaps for good. Because I could not tie my life to its owner until I processed these razored doubts and reliefs. And I could not do that here, with him. Because even now, despite everything, I loved him and wanted him. I couldn't trust myself to make the right decision while intoxicated with his presence.

He came towards me, kneeling on the rug in front of the

138

chair I sat in. He rested his head against my knee—much like he had done in York—and I allowed him, curling my fingers into tight balls so they wouldn't be tempted to twine through his thick hair.

"Let me make it up to you," he whispered, closing his eyes. "I'll do anything you want, be anything you want. But stay. Be my wife."

I was crying again. And I couldn't answer—how could I tell him that I needed to leave when I could barely stand the pain splintering across his face now? One word from him, one kiss from him, and I would fold at his feet.

His student. His wildcat. His future wife.

I said nothing as he lifted my skirts and began to lick and kiss his way up my legs to my cunt. I said nothing as he buried his face between my legs, as his own tears mingled with my arousal, and I said nothing after I came hard on his lips.

Nothing as he freed his cock and pushed inside of me, his fingers gripping me impossibly tight, as if he were afraid I'd slip away at any moment. Nothing as we rocked back and forth, as we came together in a wave of heat and shuddering.

I said nothing because I was as desperate for this as he was, this one final connection before I would go away, find my way to my aunt Esther, and sort out exactly what Mr. Markham's confession meant to me. What it meant for us.

After we finished, and he gathered me into his arms, I finally spoke. "I'm leaving," I said.

"Ivy," he said fiercely, raggedly. In that one word, I heard everything.

I looked up at him. "I love you so much."

He breathed, relief relaxing the lines around his eyes and mouth.

"But," I continued, "I need time. I need to see my family. I need to think about the lies you've told me."

He said nothing, but he buried his face in my hair and I knew he was crying.

"I'm leaving my ring on," I whispered. "But I'm saying good-bye. For now, at least."

"Can I follow you?" he asked. "Can I find you and make you mine again?"

I wanted him to. The thought of doing anything without him, being anywhere without him, made me acutely miserable. But I knew it was necessary. For both of us.

I extricated myself from his arms, hating the way I already felt cold and lonely, but still forcing myself to walk away. "I'm not using our signal, Julian. I just want some time to think. And I can't think properly around you. You . . . you consume me when we're together."

"So is that a yes, wildcat?"

I was at the door now, my hand on the knob, my mind beginning to race with how quickly I needed to pack and how I would need to find a way to Stokeleigh and how I would get word to Solicitor Wright to help arrange for my trip to London. But I turned to look back at him, my Julian, his tie unknotted, his hair unkempt, his suit rumpled from our desperate lovemaking. His green eyes, more haunted than I'd ever seen them. His soft mouth, which still made my pulse quicken. This wicked man who had brought pain to so many but had also brought me immeasurable ecstasy and happiness.

"Yes," I said quietly. "Yes, you can follow me."

He came forward, bracing his hands on either side of the door and leaning close to me. His face was inches from mine. "Then I will, wildcat. I swear."

And it was with complete honesty that I answered, "I hope you do."

He leaned in to brush his lips against mine, but I ducked away, opening the door and walking down the hallway, determined to keep my back straight and my tears at bay as I walked away from the only man I would ever love.

To Be Continued...

* * *

THANK you for reading *The Education of Ivy Leavold!* Read how Julian finally tames his wildcat in *The Punishment of Ivy Leavold*— which now includes the bonus novella *The Reclaiming of Ivy Leavold!*

The unforgettable conclusion to the Markham Hall Trilogy awaits...

I ran as far as I could, but I knew he would find me. In fact, I counted on it.

I counted on him punishing me too.

When Ivy Leavold ran away from Markham Hall on her wedding day, she knew that it wasn't the end. But what she didn't count on were the surprises, betrayals and horrors that awaited her outside of Mr. Markham's world.

As for Julian Markham, he is determined to find his bride and win her back, but when the sins of his past return with a vengeance, can he keep her safe from the most dangerous thing of all...himself?

Read the final book in the Markham Hall series now!

READY FOR THE STEAMY
CONCLUSION TO IVY AND JULIAN'S
STORY?

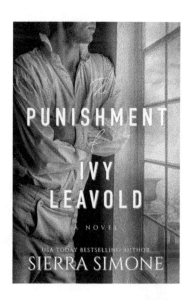

"What a really good book this was--it was so **well written and so beautifully written**! The descriptions, the smells, **the lust**...I loved Julian and Ivy!" --**Suzanne B**

"This was the best conclusion for this **wildly debauched** story!

The characters were well developed, easy to get attached too, which I truly did. **Ahh, Julian and Ivy, you will be missed!"-- Glynis T. Abermathy**

"Finally she went with her heart and what she wanted!!! **Amazing storyline**!!! Sexy &hot!!!" --**Yanixa**

Read The Punishment of Ivy Leavold now!

ALSO BY SIERRA SIMONE

Thornchapel:

A Lesson in Thorns

Feast of Sparks

Harvest of Sighs

Door of Bruises

Misadventures:

Misadventures with a Professor

Misadventures of a Curvy Girl

Misadventures in Blue

The New Camelot Trilogy:

American Queen

American Prince

American King

The Moon (Merlin's Novella)

American Squire (A Thornchapel and New Camelot Crossover)

The Priest Series:

Priest

Midnight Mass: A Priest Novella

Sinner

Saint (coming early fall 2021)

Co-Written with Laurelin Paige

Porn Star

Hot Cop

ACKNOWLEDGMENTS

A hearty thanks to the husband who makes more Hamburger Helper meals than any man should, all so I can have more time to write. An even heartier thanks to my two little ones, who suffer through Mommy's three jobs and eternally distracted brain.

To Laurelin Paige, who is brilliant and perfect, even when she's listening to me complain.

To Geneva Lee, fount of business advice and sex toy reviews. To Melanie Harlow, for hot cop sex, and to Kayti McGee for being one half of the Tits McGee equation. To Tamara Mataya, for ever so patiently editing my passive butt and for making me laugh and blush at the same time. To Erica Russikoff for giving me a final polish!

Thank you to my earliest readers, especially CD Reiss, Angie McLain, Jenna Tyler, and all the women of the Order—your genuine love for these dirty Victorians keeps me going even when the sweatpants are all dirty and the coffee is all gone. Heart eyes, motherf***er.

ABOUT THE AUTHOR

Sierra Simone is a USA Today bestselling former librarian who spent too much time reading romance novels at the information desk. She lives with her husband and family in Kansas City.

Sign up for her newsletter to be notified of releases, books going on sale, events, and other news!

www.thesierrasimone.com
thesierrasimone@gmail.com